Ode to Hope and Despair

ILANA KOVALLE

Ode to Hope and Despair

First Edition

Contents

PREFACE

"They called me bubbly, unaware, that in the winter of my soul, bubbles don't survive."

Ode to Hope and Despair is a compilation of pieces written mostly under the influence of my darkest hours, spent at the bottom of a dungeon created by my own mind. However, even in the depths of the abyss, I still caught glimpses of the stars, which had to shine brighter than ever to pierce through the dense darkness. And shine bright they did. After all, what is Despair if not Hope through the looking glass, and what is Hope if not Despair reflected in a funhouse mirror? Where there is one, there will always be the other, just a foot away, ready to take over at any mis-/right-step. And life is but a continuous attempt at the fine balance.

I have spent years building up shells of fake identity to fit into the world I thought was not for me. Now, by means of writing, I'm peeling away layers of this shell and, instead of trying to be part of the world, I finally let the world become part of me. I don't need to wait for my life to be free of depressive episodes to start living. And recurrence of those episodes doesn't put my life on hold. It's all part of it.

This book is both for those dealing with depression and for their loved ones - to provide hope to the former and insight to the latter. The reason I wanted this book to exist was to help the former become more familiar with their own mind and help the latter better understand the mind of the former. There is quite a bit of relief in the knowledge that someone else is going through a similar experience, that we are not alone in our struggles. Depression grows its largest fangs when lurking in the shadows of rejection to which it has been exiled. So, the normalization of it as a widely shared experience that can (and should) be openly discussed is a way to cleanse those shadows with light and fire.

Ode to Hope and Despair travels through its pages from darkness to light and turns that very travel into a lighthouse, which beacons reminders during recurring episodes of depression about their impermanence. These can be rather important reminders, since in the grip of depression, the memory of the past flickers of lights and the hope for future ones can get tempered and undermined, falling beyond the reach of the painful reality of the moment.

This book is also a testament to the big lesson I learned - that depression is a part of me, and while it might be only one part of my whole, denying its existence stands in the way of true self-acceptance. So this compilation is a process of integration of all of my parts that I previously rejected. It is my attempt to introduce the me of my dark days to the me of my good days, because where there is one, the other isn't, and I'd very much like for them to finally make peace with each other's existence. Ever since I've gone on the path of accepting all of me and embracing depression, its bouts have been getting softer and kinder, and who knows, soon enough I might have less of me in my head and more room for the rest of the world. So, in a way, this book is my declaration of peace - peace amidst all my selves, after decades of brutal inner wars.

...but when I looked up

the hand that held me

was mine...

when your hopeless being is craving for healing,
but old wounds still bleed when you least expect;
all you wonder is whether you are safe in your wreck.

...You know shadow as absence of light, but could light be known without it?...

When you fall asleep crying, always thinking of dying,
and your mind imagines all the ways to end it;
when your wishful thinking is sending you sinking,
and dreams bring despair 'cause you lack what it takes;
all you wish - to one day find mercy in the death breaks.

...Can self-disdain be disguised hubris, or can hubris pretend as insecurity?...

When instead of inspiring, you send yourself miring
in your self-deprecation and jealousy bog;
when you can't help concurring with the blames your mind's pouring –
that you're a damn homoclite with nothing to give;
all you hope is delusion where you're more than you believe.

...Are you the darkness swallowing others, or has the darkness swallowed you alone?...

When you cannot stop hurting, as your self-loathe is burning,
tarnished by self-pity that you sometimes feel;
when you can't help agreeing with the voice that is screaming
that you're just nothing and should not be alive;
all you want is oblivion 'cause no meaning - no life.

...But if you'd never known the twinge of hatred, would you be capable of compassion?...

SOAP BUBBLES

I've spent January blowing bubbles,
watching them wade into the waste of the elements,
watching them crash into the cruel breath of winter,
winter so hardened with jealousy for spring,
that it steals spring's citrus green and turns it into the lime of envy,
winter so struggling to find content in being itself,
that it slacks the stolen lime into self-rejecting snow,
and goes around saying that to live on,
the bubbles are requemed to reject themselves and harden too -
and so thirsty for life they are,
that without hesitation, they shift their essence,
turning into icy spheres,
which then crash into the ground
and break open the lives that can't survive
without their shell.

What do you do when reality bursts,
bursts like a bubble, leaving soap around?
What do you do when your soul hurts
from the soap in your eyes, with no water found?

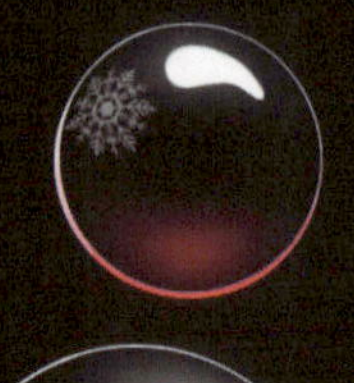

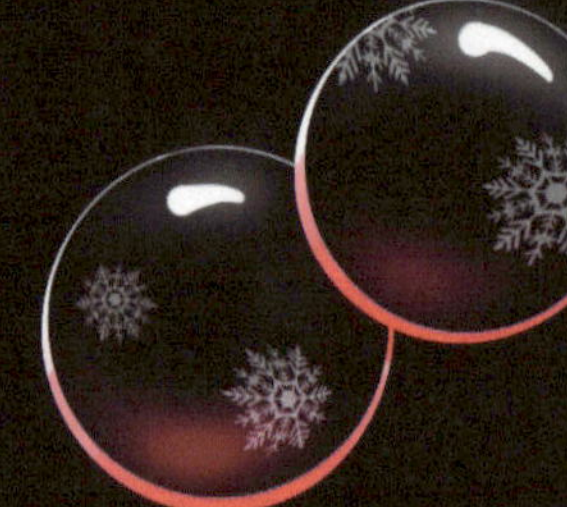

When soap bubbles burst in their natural form,
I never think of them dying a hundred thousand times -
in every tiny droplet that sparkles the brightest in its final wink at the sun -
there's no thought of that being their end,
because death is rough and gruesome and cannot be lovely;
but when bubbles freeze and in their freezing break,
little is ephemeral about that end -
be it the icy body parts of a once bubble
that turn still water in an instant,
or the tiny little cloud of a final breath,
visible for just that instant before becoming air.

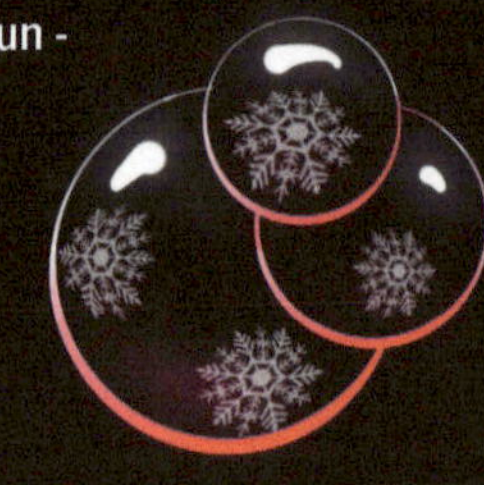

And then I see it -
the air around me is nothing
but a graveyard of soap bubbles
that have bought their beauty
with the brevity of their life;
yet tragically, they were never aware
of the beauty they possessed.

SLUDGE SOLDIERS

Nothing can be done about the currents of sludge-
tinted soldiers swarming inside my head,
floods of dark bodies, whose only goal is
self-destruction through drowning in,
self-destruction through drowning out.

They roll in circle motions, like moon around Earth
from too far to too close and back again,
each of them wielding spathas in place of guns -
of the ninth wave's size and weighted by sins;
each spatha has a handle, yet the hands choose to grip
straight at the blades, cutting through their flesh,
making hands bleed, grinding right at the bones -
the more they thrust at others, the more they harm themselves.

But I never see the blood 'cause the blades are made of
the ominous scarlet, confusing me each time -
in this burning red, attention screams, alarm whispers,
as if giving me a hint of yet another invasion,
as if commanding to run, other options doomed;
yet that confusion is only momentary,
as I get swamped by the black and red tsunami,
which I always see coming but never succeed
at running away from, no matter the warnings;
and ruby spathas turn from conspicuous red flags
into mocking twinkling glares in the bloody mouth
of my insatiate self-hate, sinned in Gula and Tristitia -
black oceans that fill me within and without.

No, nothing can be done about the torrents of sludge
soldiers always fighting inside my head:
I painted them silt, gave them their damn blades,
I showed them my wreckage, trained them to be tsunami;
now I walk the plank, asking for mercy, forgetting
that mercy's the one thing I never taught them.

...i've always so craved attention
that I turned my whole life into a stage,
with myself the only person in the audience,
a hater.

FIREFLIES

i don't have enough warmth in my blood to warm myself, let alone others -
so cold inside that the cold outside is warmer;

yet when i let blood to check its temperature, steam rises from the ruby liquid,
boiling so bright, it draws people in, fireflies to flames;

yet the boiling is so fervent that it's gone within a second, dissolved in blushing fog,
leaving people feeling fooled as they don't get the warmth they've come for,

leaving people unawares that they've escaped getting scalded -

after all, enamored with flames, fireflies light up to their death
and turn to cinder before they even know they're dying.

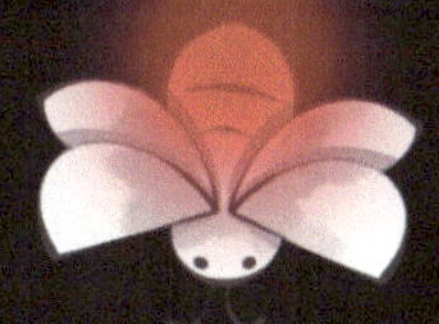

A FEW SIGNS SOMETHING IS WRONG

The third time I know something is wrong, I am nineteen:
my mind prompts me to feed chunks
of physical pain to my mental vipers -
all it wants me to do is to stop
the cognitive dissonance,
where the teeming reptile lair in its depths
somehow exists without matching crawlers on my skin,
and since I can't purify the inner bog into the outer sea,
I must destroy the sea,
turn it into a swamp,
or dry it completely.

and I'm an anaconda that's devoured her own bane,
and is now gnawing at her intestines,
and all she's left to do is to attack her own body,
bite and chew at her own flesh,
for one of the bites must hit the target and destroy
the predator inside until at last she sees
that this whole time, she sought to swallow her own tail,
choking on it, convulsing,
yet unable to spit it out -
the predator and the prey united,
until both are no more.

The second time I suspect something is wrong, I am sixteen:
friends prompt me to slither out
of the embrace of my cave,
all they want me to do is to bare
my fangs and expose
the grimmer shades of my thoughts to light
to see if they might
catch on fire.

I guess water cleanses until it drowns,

....depression has a curious sense of humor....

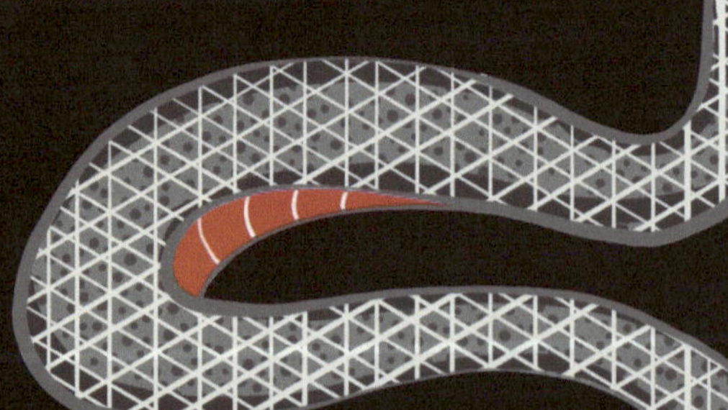

I guess fire cleanses until it incinerates,

and I'm a chameleon attempting to change
the pigment of my skin to neutral, as I bask
to emit warmth and not just leech on others' colors;
when that fails, I peel skin, turn it to leather,
trade for carapace of vulnerability,
ready to stand without my camouflage.
Too soon - the carapace isn't strong enough,
and my body slips out of it -
an ostrich nestling oozing out of a broken egg,
metamorphosis unfinished.
"You have no right to be miserable" - I know
"You make God angry by being so ungrateful" - I know
"You have too skinny a body, too light a skin,
too loving a family, too decent a job, too good a life" - I know
I have all the wings I need to fly, but in the end
an ostrich is still a reptile, and aren't reptiles born to crawl?

....if only happiness was a checklist....

The first time I should have known something is wrong, I am thirteen:
mom prompts me towards our hallway mirror -
all she wants me to do is to perk up and squeak to myself
"I love you. You're beautiful."

I guess love cleanses until it suffocates,

and the scales of my vocal cords break,
turning my throat into a piton that's lost control -
its own muscle turning against it,
as if hoping to squeeze the words out of me,
or strangle me with the weight of those words,
whichever comes first.
It isn't so much that I can't hiss a lie,
but that I realize that lying is the only option available,
I don't remember what I see in the mirror,
but I can't forget the cascade of venom
seeping out of my eyes,
its bites on my skin serving as consolation -
pitons aren't supposed to be venomous.
But this one is.

...some beasts are simply not hatched to be pets...

PAINFUL

Painful,
when there is nothing to look for,
and emptiness in your heart's core
bites hard at your will.
> Painful,
> when settlement is your one choice,
> indifference cracks in your voice -
> all hope does is kill...

Painful,
when you want something to wish for,
yet that wishing turns your heart sore;
feelings sink in void.
> Painful,
> when defeat's all that accepts you...
> still haunted by the chance that you blew,
> but hope's not destroyed.

Painful,
and from that pain you are weeping
but still spend your life just creeping -
can't fly with torn wings.
> Painful,
> when purposelessness seeps within you,
> happy-hurt-content's preferred queue -
> hope is full of stings.

Painful,
with no reason to keep fighting,
void of oblivion's inviting -
you're a shell of past life.
> Painful,
> but pain is better than nothing,
> even when hope's disgusting,
> it keeps you alive...

...I'm treading through the ocean of despair,
with hope - a candle in my hand
that spills enough light to make me aware
I haven't yet merged with the ocean around.

HAPPY LITTLE ISLAND

I wish you'd met me when I was
still a happy little island
scented by a pearly lilac
with a unicorny heart;
when that heart was young and whole
and not the mess that it is now,
not this butchered hackled mess,
I tried to mend so many times
that drying blood on all my stitches
turns them now into tentacles -
a unicorn before, an octopus now...

I wish you'd met me when I was
a cerulean balloon,
full of sparkling soap bubbles,
ringing laughters, flashing smiles,
and not the bitter fumes of pain
that are too heavy for balloons;
so hammered down to the ground
mine now draggles, pondering whether
there really was a time when it could fly.

I wish you'd met me when I was
one naive and harmless cloud
charged with dreams and inspiration
that loved the world with all its essence,
still untouched by cynicism;
and hypocrites are fairy tales
that soon enough it was to live through,
that soon enough it was to turn to;
the soft and clueless cloud
let its air be displaced
with a shine of quicksilver,
which stole life from all its cells
and broke it in plumbum flakes
scattered now all around.

I wish you'd met me when I was
still a little sweet Miss Sunshine,
who cared not of her own troubles
as long as she could help another,
who cared so much for others
that helping them was all she wanted -
in empathy her heart rejoiced.
With what you see now I know
it is a challenge to believe
that Miss Sunshine once was me...

It's really too bad you missed her.

I'm sorry you missed her.

UNEXIST

The world won't even pause,
when i stop to be;
insignificant...
i live with made up meanings.

All memory'll fade out,
as if i never was;
replaceable...
i'm wasting this existence.

So little to leave behind -
will you remember me?
unnecessary...
Have i ever touched your heart?

Keep up the struggle, it'll ease -
you keep on telling me;
exhausted...
But why do i have to struggle?

Why live on in cruel hope,
waiting for small wonders?
Desperate...
i just wish to unexist.

You say you'd die for me,
so i must live for you;
illogical -
why can't i just die for me?...

PLEASE, DON'T

Leave me behind, don't drag me along,
let me get lost, make my own mistakes;
you're a beautiful soul, so worthy and strong,
and i'm such a burden, always slamming your breaks.

Why are you so kind? Your eyes must be failing, if you do not see
i am the last person to deserve your care.
i have nothing to offer in return - all i'm filled with
is darkness and tears; i'm just a damp dark
piece of crap, but you treat me
like i'm worthy of something, of something good and wonderful,
like you.
Why do you care so? It's wrong that you should pour
your radiant energy into my black hole -
it won't fix me.
Your strength won't boost mine, and your care won't make me whole.
It's so wrong that you should waste
your kindness on a lost cause.
Please don't.
You can do so much more with it, instead of exhausting it on me.
i'm sorry i'm such a waste;
i'm sorry your kindness compels you to try to help me;
i'm so sorry i make you feel hopeless, even angry
for being unable to help me;
i have more dark of despair than you have light of strength.
i'm sorry but please leave before i ruin you too.
Please, don't be so good to me...

Leave me behind, stop trying to help -
i'm a hopeless case, a drag on your life;
walk without footprints, a ghost in the shell,
i spread cold and darkness, toxic to all alive.

SHOULD'VE KNOWN BETTER

You told me to lift my heart's curtain
because you were my good friend,
and i had nothing to fear,

for you'd never betray me.

You gave me a cue to open up
because you cast yourself as
reliable and worthy of trust -

such a true leading man.

You had little idea yet how hard
that scene, that action was for me,
and you started to resent

my taking so much time.

You wanted to know me better,
although i warned against it,
as i knew you had no clue

who hid behind the role i played.

You wanted me to trust you
for the sake of your own ego,
though you honestly believed

you were doing it for me.

It was then little surprise,
as i cracked open my heart,
bringing its darkness on stage,

you jumped back, retreat in the eyes.

It was then little surprise,
as i slightly shifted my mask,
letting you glimpse the tormented face,

you wished to forget it, unsee.

You truly did not know
that at this performance, broken
trust was the fourth wall that revealed

my true colors, or rather their absence.

You truly knew so little
seeing me with a made-up halo,
blind to my struggles to climb up

to your suspended disbelief.

i should have known better
and saved you the embarrassment
of forgetting your lines, as i moved the drapes

back in their place, rehearsal over.

i should have known better
and foreseen that your script had no room
for the bleakness of my heart and mind -

after all, it is my farce, and mine alone.

i should have known better
and hoped not for a callback -
foul phantom outside her opera,

should've long since learned her lesson.

WORST THING

'Cause the worst thing
that you can do
to someone you're
trying to help through
some tough crap
is to blame them
for not improving
despite your presence
despite your efforts
so they feel worse
for letting you
down

'Cause the worst thing
that you can do
to someone you're
trying to help through
betrayal is to
demand that they
trust you 'cause you
claim you're worthy
of their trust
and call you a friend
simply 'cause that's
what you think you are

'Cause the worst thing
that you can do
to someone who's
trying to help you through
an illness is
to not get better
so you feel pressured
to fake the better
but it's not fair
to you or them

There are hundreds of voices screaming in my head:
that my life isn't worthy, and I'm better off dead,
that I don't have what it takes to be happy, to be whole,
that I wasn't born to fly - all I'm destined is to crawl.

SNOWFLAKE

A snowflake gets tangled in her lashes,
and a second later it is freed
by a soft clash with the eyelid;
and she feels it rushing down
the hill of her cheekbone
into the curve of her dimple,

"You're not my tear, but you're welcome
to join me on this sweet morning -
the *tickles* in my nose catch me
between sneezing and laughing,
as tears welcome the brightness of the world around."

* * *

A snowflake falls onto her cheek,
and a moment later a warm stream emerges
from the tiny creation of the cold;
and she feels it rushing down
to crush on the cliff of her collar bone,
as it changed its very nature,

"You're not my tear, but you're welcome
to die on my cheek all the same tonight -
my cheeks are very good for dying on,
unlit by broken streetlights, two *graveyards* of lost hopes,
with tears mourning every last one of them."

The snowflakes did not know
that between the *tickles* and the *graveyards*
stood a single night.

HURT ME

i'm right here -
        just turn your head, stretch your hand,
                grab my throat,
                        suffocate till understand.
Make me cry,
        cut up my heart, make me bleed;
                i deserve
                        to ache - i'm a useless weed.
Shake me hard.
        scratched off soul and burned up feet -
                i can't walk -
                        masochist, won't even plead.
Do me wrong -
        my heart's on fire, bound by ice...
                Please, align
                        my inner hell with surface vice.

So hurt me till i choke,
        hurt me till i cry;
                tie my heart with ropes,
                        squeeze it till it's dry.
You know that i want it;
            it's easier this way -
                    i'm numb when i am whole,
                        alive just when in pain...
                            Alive through bits of pain.

TOO MANY i'S

i have
too many I's in my head,
i think
way too much of myself,
i want
to be anyone else
who's better than this.
> but it's all
> one vicious circle that
> i can't get out of -
> i'm running around,
> complaining, but doing
> nothing to change.
> > so when i
> > ask for your help,
> > i expect that you will
> > lie to me. lie to me! tell me
> > i'm beautiful,
> > funny, talented, and smart.
> but that lie
> might not even be enough,
> unless you add that i am
> better than her,
> smarter than him,
> funnier than them,
> more talented than any.
yes, i have
too many i's in my head,
and unless i'm better than
somebody else,
i won't feel good,
won't feel right,
so misery i might
deserve after all...

CEMETERY

My mind is a cemetery -

a mass grave of feelings unrequited,
a tomb of memories forgotten,
a memorial of dreams aborted,

where discomfort justifies
cutting people off,
cutting hearts up.

My mind is a dump -

a dungeon of spilled regret,
where deceived hopes rot into despair,

where kindness is abandoned
for sake of convenience,

and basic human decency
is the subject of a joke.

For a little bit, I believed that I succeeded at helping my mind give up the habit of vividly picturing my death at least twice a day - be it a promisingly short fall from the 19th floor of my flat on the parking lot underneath, or a shorter yet fall from the platform on the tracks before an incoming train.
And when I say 'vividly' I mean I can feel the dryness in my eyes from falling through all that air.
And when I say 'vividly' I mean I can hear the cracking of my breaking bones on the rails.

For a little bit, I believed that you would never forget about my mind's habit of searching for ways to hurt me and relishing in any pain it caused me. But you did forget and couldn't see how my mind applauded when your greedy fingers broke into my innocence. You did forget and didn't see how my mind laughed at me with "serves you right" and "you deserve this".
Yet unlike you, it shut up at the sudden wake of reason from the desperate cries of the little girl inside and apprehended the wrongness of its collusion with you.
Yet unlike you, it shut up and never deformed the words "I love you" into an excuse.

For a little bit, I believed that I could wake up from the nightmare and laugh it off as my mind's habitually twisted sense of humor. A nightmare where I'm a mute screaming and pleading, with the sounds never finding escape from my lips: they're trapped in my throat, echo in my ears, deafen my mind, amplify my feelings... "no, don't, no, please, don't touch me, don't touch..." these mute screams... there are too many of them, filling my head and emptying it at the same time... my mind's on the verge of exploding... "No, please, stop touching me..."

But why won't I wake up?!

ENTITLED

No *you* didn't have the right to use me like that
       i knew *you* felt broken so i tried to help
       i knew *you* spilled out anger and self-hate
       so i let myself be the outlet for *you*
       but i do admit i used to believe that
       outlet would mean something else entirely

No *you* didn't have the right to treat me like that
       i thought *you* felt shattered and i did all to heal *you*
       i thought *you* just needed love care and some patience
       so i gave *you* all i had but it wasn't enough
       as *your* rage needed a special kind of punchbag
       and i was too naive to hope i could change that in *you*

No *you* didn't have the right to break me like that
       i was just a scared girl who looked up to *you* for strength
       i was just a little broken thing myself   lonely   alone
       but i still worked so hard to make things easier for *you*
       first i swallowed my words then my pride to make *you* smile
       but i had no clue how much *your* good spirits would cost me

no. *you* had no. fucking. right. to trap me. like that.
       but all too soon assault and apology were a norm
       and all too soon i became convinced that i deserved it
       you marred my body and so my mind found escape in numbness
       you were the good guy and i was scared to break the illusion
       i was lonely with others but alone with *you* i was dead

OATH

You broke me for breaking *you*
for breaking me for breaking *you*;
You hurt *yourself* for hurting me;
and for hurting *you*, i hurt me too,
but

i won't give *you* a blade and ask
you to grant me absolution
by plunging it into my chest -
i know *you* won't do it.

i won't tell *you* i still hope
for release from the regrets
in the promise of oblivion -
it won't do *you* any good.

i won't try to explain to others
how much i hurt
(for what I did to *you*, from what *you* did to me)
because pain is relative,
and i worked hard to earn mine.

i won't excuse my actions with *yours*
or *yours* with mine, though tempting -
torturer and tortured,
they can have one face.

i won't defend myself from those
who pass final judgement -
my tears and sobs are selfish acts,
and i must own my mistakes.

i won't hide behind the little girl -
innocent and insecure...
i am just another monster,
who received what she deserved.

WISH

I wish my mind could erase
all those nights when I betrayed it,
all those times when I degraded
myself for others' sake.

I wish my heart would stop to startle
upon each memory dyed despise,
upon each flashback of the vice
I forced myself to go through.

I wish my heart would learn forgiveness
for my frightened lack of action,
for my freeze-and-sob reaction
in place of fight and yelled-out 'No'.

I wish my mind could forget
the touch, the dread, the trust, its break,
the cries, the blame, the guilt, its ache;
I wish I had protected me
better...

DYING SUN

Scarlet sun quiet dying in fire
pleads mercy of ruthless night;
rays of blood freezing in mire
trace the end in snow's slight.

Crying sun panicked drowns in blood.
It knows, squirms, but can't understand -
moon's mashing her love with mud
dooms her to lose both heart and hand.

Looking cold at sun's gasps for air,
moon laughs, immune to the guilty feel -
the one to blame, yet watched with no care,
as sun, in death, turned to onyx steel.

TRUST

There should be legal safety limits

on how much trust one can vest in a person;

ignorance shouldn't be cuddled,
but maybe trust could come with explicit disclaimers and warnings,

as the trusting might need to be protected from themselves.

Trust is the priciest of gifts,
and I felt blessed to have the means to grant it;

some gifts can be under- and over-priced at the same time.

Trust is the deadliest of weapons,
and I readily armed you with it to keep me you safe;

some weapons can be used to re-distribute safety unevenly.

The one I trusted the most to protect me from harm
harmed me the most in the end,

for I all but showed you the best way to do it.

FACETS OF ACCEPTANCE

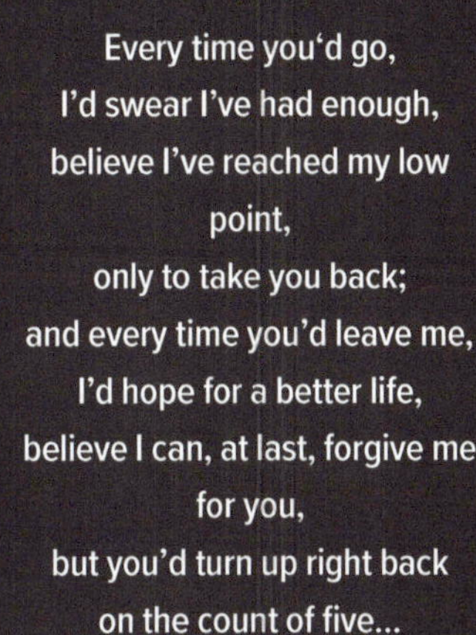

Every time you'd go,
I'd swear I've had enough,
believe I've reached my low
point,
only to take you back;
and every time you'd leave me,
I'd hope for a better life,
believe I can, at last, forgive me
for you,
but you'd turn up right back
on the count of five...

You made me feel   so ashamed;
you made me feel   like I was to blame;
you made me feel   like to you I was indebted,
like I had to give myself up,   like I had to break myself up
to make it up to you...
You made me feel   like I had to hurt as much
as I thought   I made you hurt...

...Now you're holding my heart in your ice-cold hands,
it's burning your skin, but you won't let it fall.
Yet my crying heart is being hurt by your touch:
in this game we cannot win - you've carved out my heart and left me a hole...

...Forgive isn't forget,
but someday I know I will
let go of all regret,
grow numb to the memory;
forgive isn't move on,
but I have learned to not stand still;
nothing lasts forever -
it's the curse of this world
and its blessing.

STRANGERS

I wish we could go back to being just strangers;
strangers who haven't yet harmed one another,
who haven't seen that hope can be cruel,
who don't expect or even know
that the world can tumble down
with one wrong word or act.

I wish we could go back to being just free;
free as in you from me and me from guilt,
free as in seeing our future in others,
free as in absent torment of the mind
about what once happened
and what could never be.

Sometimes I wish we could just unmeet;
unmeet and not have to force acceptance,
unmeet and escape thoughts of rejection,
unmeet and avoid feeling indebted
for unreturned feelings
that cannot be subdued.

I wish we could go back to being just free;
free as in you needn't me to be happy,
free as in I worry not how you feel,
free as in we don't dream of undoing
the hell that each of us has
thrown the other in.

I wish we could go back to being just strangers;
strangers who are yet to be stabbed by betrayal,
who haven't yet learned that trust can't be trusted,
who still haven't viewed themselves
as "lacking" or "damaged"
because of each other.

IMSICKOFMYSELF

Involuntarily prodding into the night,
Moving through the thick plain of the void,
Softly whimpering in the idle echoes of life,
Insolence pretending innocence and virtue,
Calling out others's faults but blind to her own,
Knowing of the imminent failure yet going anyway,
Oppressor and oppressed in one face,
Forcing colors to merge, light turning dark,
Merely wishing to somehow be better,
Yet wishfully thinking making a full circle,
Slaying intentions in their very birth,
Eliminating urges before they turn desires,
Living a half life, giving up before trying,
F**king up already by not even starting.

...I'm wading through the howling wind
of self-doubts I imagined,
of judgements on me inflicted,
of opinions I should've long convicted;
lost in expectations for me built up,
in knowingly getting into a trap,
in guilt for finding enough nerve,
to complain about what I don't even deserve...

LARK

She has the sweetest smile -
the smile that invites you to smile along,
that makes you guilty for not listening,
as jingles you hear in that smile
melt away all you thought was wrong.

She has the brightest eyes -
the eyes whose laughing twinkles are larks unchained,
and seconds later, she looks in earnest,
serene and carefree, those eyes
shine with trust like fireflies in rain.

She has the warmest heart -
the heart that gathers all by a fireplace
to sit around, differences aside,
and it makes you feel like home,
affection breathing from each face.

She has the sweetest smile -
the sweet that's only born from once known ache
and a wish to be a soothing balm -
if not heals, that smile comforts
with swishy touch of a small bird.

She has the brightest eyes -
the bright that only comes from inhaled dark,
color of the universe in mourning,
with unshed tears turned to stars
that glisten now in moveless stark.

She has the warmest heart -
the warm that steams from spilled out blood
burning feverishly in fading life,
she spills more, burning brighter,
as lark's sweetest trill turns to thud.

MUTE AND BLIND

It's like I am in a tunnel,
and they keep telling me
there will be light at its end,
but they don't know I am blind.

It's like I look at the night sky
and pick a star to wish upon,
and be my guiding light in life,
but I don't know it's long dead.

It's like my heart is slit by paper
that you once gave me as a tissue;
now you hand cotton, say it's sterile,
but you don't know it's fiberglass.

It's like I am standing by a fire;
its crackle heating up my bones;
its smoke patting down my cheeks;
but I know not I stand in ashes.

It's like my soul is in free fall
through the abyss of my mind,
and my heart's caught in barbed wires,
but you know not and keep on pulling.

It's like I'm under tonnes of water,
so deep - I can't tell where's surface;
"Cry for help!" They're chanting, muffled,
but they know not that I am mute.

*...And they just make me feel so guilty
for not being bigger than I am,
for lacking the ambition to be bigger,
for finding comfort in my own size.*

DOLL

One   sad   broken doll   in the showcase;
given the front seat to observe the world,
given the front seat to be watched by it -
she desired neither.

One   sad   broken doll   on the windowsill;
looking silly with one eye half open,
looking crazy with one eye half closed -
she was incomplete.

One   mad   broken doll   on the windowsill;
hollow inside and she knew it,
hollow so much that she didn't care -
she dreamt of not being.

One   mad   lonely doll   on the windowsill;
belonged with the world that refused her,
belonged to the world that wasn't hers -
she had nobody.

One   mad   lonely soul on the windowsill;
gave up the life as it passed by,
gave up on ever being its part -
she felt like a weed.

One   mad   lonely soul   on the windowsill;
sought a reason to not be ok,
sought to excuse her default pain,
she knew she was wrong.

One   mad   broken soul   on the windowsill;
filled with solitude of the crowd,
filled with deep absence of the light,
she echoed silence.

One   sad   broken soul   on the windowsill;
wishing to hurt to feel something,
wishing to feel herself alive,
she was always numb.

One   sad   broken soul   in the showcase;
cried at the smile of a little girl,
cried at the warmth she never knew,
she learned sting of hope.

> *A doll with a soul one day might discover freedom,*
> *a soul trapped in a doll might forget freedom one day.*

DOLL (reprise)

"Daddy, this doll is broken."
The doll hit the floor. She was used to being dropped. The doll knew she was broken, in her memory she always had been actually. She just couldn't remember what broke her. Or when. Or how.
"It's okay sweetheart, don't touch it, somebody will pick it up and put it away. What nonsense to display broken dolls in the showcase!"

The doll didn't wince. The blanket of dust that she landed in seemed to regard her as an equal, and she was afraid to break that illusion.

She didn't give a sign of frustration or anger at being dropped, even though she was full of both. But more than anything, she was filled with hatred. She hated herself for being broken, for being incomplete, being wrong. She hated herself for feeling angry with all the girls who had dropped her upon noticing her defect. She knew she was angry with them for not accepting her with her faults, yet she couldn't justify that anger in her little head, as she
also knew that they were under no obligation to accept her regardless. And so she hated herself for being so unjustly angry.

The doll didn't look. Her eyes remained half-open, but she willed herself into blindness, hoping that not seeing meant she couldn't be seen. Yet she still felt the judging stares, even as she chose to not see them.

She hated herself even more for being jealous of the other, more complete, dolls. She was torn between wanting to be happy for them - their beauty and good fortune - and feeling horribly inadequate upon perceiving the vast contrast existing between them and her. She knew how to see the best in others yet only focused on the worst in her. Still, it wasn't that she wanted those dolls to lose their perfection and become like her; it was simply that every observance of their unmatched loveliness made her exorbitantly more aware of her own lack thereof, of her insufficiency, her incompleteness. She wished to be happy for them, but that wish was poisoned by envy. And so she hated herself for being so susceptible to the ugly envy.

The doll didn't sigh. Her eyes unwillingly spotted all previous locations, where she disturbed the layer of dust with her uninvited presence, wondering at the dust's patience.

Most of all, she hated herself for hating herself. For being so powerless before the overwhelming negative feeling that swallowed her into its icy slimy darkness. She wanted to be strong and full of sunshine to bring happiness to others, yet her default state seemed to permanently be the opposite. She wanted to care, to help, to give joy, but she was too broken for any of that. She was too full of hatred and despair, too detached from her wishes to even try to realize them. All she could feel was exhaustion - she was tired from people;

frustration - she was upset with the world; hatred - she was fed up with herself for being so pitiful, so pathetic, for being a weed unworthy of grooming, a weed unworthy of blooming.

An accidental shove by a stranger's boot sent the doll gliding across the floor, until she came to a muffled stop in the long skirts of another girl. The doll resigned to her fate. She no longer even cared enough for polite lies, such as friendly smiles or, at least, smiley eyes. Her eyes now were a reflection of her hollowness inside, and she made no effort to hide it. On the opposite, she let the cold and hurt and bitterness seep through them. She thought with a note of gloomy satisfaction that, at least, this time, the "drop" would be well-deserved...

...The little girl perplexedly looked around, then lowered her eyes to the strange object that scored in her skirts out of nowhere. Her small hand carefully raised what happened to be a little doll. It was a strange doll though, different from all the other dolls she'd seen. And it looked so sad that the girl's heart pinched, and unable to contain herself, the girl sat on the floor and wept. And as she wept, she squeezed the doll in the tightest embrace she was capable of, pressing it against her heart, and letting out all the unshed tears of hurt and loneliness she'd seen in the
doll's eyes.

"I'm so sorry..." whispered the girl,
and in her words there was an apology for all
the world. But more than anything, there
was acceptance, there was admittance
and welcome to the world that had
previously so stubbornly kept on casting
the doll away. The little girl was
suddenly a big and loving universe, and
the broken doll...

...For the first time in her life the doll
forgot that she was broken. For the first
time, she had hope to be complete again
some day...

...*for only the heart that's been maimed by despair*
knows the true beauty of hope.

ODE TO DESPAIR

Every single day I whisper lies in my own ears -
that there's something bigger that's still waiting for me;
that there's something more that I am meant to be;
I'm searching hard but can't find what that is.

They say life should be easy: if it's not - you live it wrong;
but my easy is empty, as I spend it alone.
There's no more answers; I'm confused, I am lost,
as the one thing I want to live for hurts me the most.

.

Like a bird with cutoff wings, like a painter with no sight,
like a writer with broken fingers, I'm a dreamer whose dream lost its light;
an artist who has just started, yet frustration already built up...
I've let down my dream when I parted "I want" from "I can" and gave up.

When your mind is full of music that you're unable to express,
wouldn't it be much more humane all that music to simply suppress?
Suppress and not distress that you can't share it with the world;
suppress and put the ache to a stop - my dream was ready, when I was not.

So every time that I get up, I have to fight off despair;
'cause what I want to be I'm not, and somehow that isn't unfair;
and every time I go to bed, I try so hard to not cry;
'cause what I want to be I can't, yet that each time I deny.

But what if the world is an orchestra,
and my heart is an instrument
with its own unique sound,
whose beat already fits beautifully with the rest?...

SNOWFLAKE (reprise)

Sapphire-ebon snow swirls
on monochrome background;

my dandelion hair is
peppered with snowflakes;

in their sable shimmer,
there's a distant whisper,

"You're gonna be alright -
life's such a lovely place."

PASSERBY

But who am I today -
another blur that you'll pass by without seeing;
another story that you'll never get to hear;
another hurt that you'll choose to overlook,
as it affects you not?
    Maybe, if you looked into my eyes,
    just for a moment raising yours to see,
    to see, not look - to really see -
    you would be blessed with a "Good morning!"
    because it is a lovely morning!
    I woke up, I'm breathing, and so are you,
    and I hope you enjoy your day.
        Or maybe, if you ever dared
        to steal a glimpse of what my eyes are telling,
        you'd hear an apology
        for not having the words of "Good day!"
        standing ready,
        as it hasn't been the easiest of days,
        and I could really use a friendly face,
        if only for a second spent in passing you.
            And maybe you would choose
            to support me with a smile -
            my favorite smile of sonder (acknowledgement
            of the beauty of another human life),
            and you'd see how that one smile
            turns the apology in my eyes
            into gratitude.
                And maybe, if I unlearned to hide my eyes,
                and had a smile of support
                available for my own self, to prop me up,
                maybe then I wouldn't be in such a dire
                need of your confirmation of my existence,
                maybe then I wouldn't see myself as just a blur -

                                    a passerby
                                    in my own life.

TEARS

Did you know that tears can leave scars?
Scars so deep, they burn to charcoal
their path on the surface of the heart,
as they swarm around it,
pleading to be let in;
and when they fail to find an entrance,
they decide to drill one in,
scalding everything with salt.

I never realized how sharp tears can bite,
until I kept my eyes
watered by them for so long
that the saline carved away
the tender exterior of the skin,
clawing into the flesh and blazing through it;
so that when my eyes finally dried out,
they were surrounded by nothing but heaps
of flaking skin and salt crystals.

Did you know that tears can heal wounds?
Wounds so old, they became polar stars,
keeping you aware of the one direction,
you never want to find yourself in again;
but tears fill those wounds with warmth,
and bring the astray polar stars
back home.

PUZZLE

Every presence in her life is a piece of the puzzle her life is made of.

Some people fit perfectly,
even when she doesn't expect them to;
others don't belong in the picture,
however hard she squeezes them in spare slots;
those spare slots better left unfilled,
as they don't distort the image -
just breathe possibility into it.

There are spaces filled with saturated hollow -
lost puzzle pieces that can't be replaced:
some of these pieces used to possess the warmest colors in the picture,
until they were lost and in their loss, burned off to black;
some of these pieces used to shine with the fiercest glow in the picture,
until they were lost and in their loss, frostbit to black;

So now, all they are is black -
the black that tactlessly demands attention,
that can't be overlooked or unseen...
that stares back from anywhere in the picture,
always reminding of the missing presence.
When that blackness first appears, it absorbs the brightness
of all the other colors in the picture.
and the picture, as it was once meant to be,
has lost its chance to ever be complete,
overwritten with these breaths of black fire,
with the fingerprints of black frost.

And as she looks at the puzzle,
knowing that she can never mend its black wounds,
she wants to shut her eyes and never see the puzzle again.
Yet as the puzzle keeps growing,
she soon learns to not reject the crippled image,
but to embrace it exactly for the beauty inherent in its black scars...

I've said goodbye so many times,
I should by now be immune
to all that sadness, useless cries...
But each time, they strikes anew.

I've said goodbyes my whole life,
I know no other way, it's now a habit...
Instead of fighting, I just quit the strife -
I'm one small sad silly goodbye addict.

IGNORANCE IS SWEET

I'm ten and it's Christmas Eve,
it's only five, but the sun has set,
and the warmth of our kitchen light,
is all sprinkled with the cookie scent.

I'm eighteen and an egoist,
I do not see what is happening -
illusions melt, with them my naïveté;
one can be innocent in ignorance.

I'm twenty five and full of despair -
ignorance and innocence both are gone;
my world is crumbling and I just can't bear
to watch my Christmas cookie come undone.

They won't hear my plea, they don't hear my prayer,
and I'm now too old to not understand;
I wish that my tears still held any weight,
just like when I was little and they really cared...

...And I want to run, but I make myself stay,
I force me to listen and even speak up -
one tiny difference I still hope to make,
even though I just wish their fighting would stop.

Now I'm caught in the middle,
I'm on both their sides, and I side with no one;
it's all up to them, but they have given up,
so all I have left is to live in the past,

where I am just ten, and maybe they fight,
but I know nothing, I'm not a peacemaker -
only a girl, with a cookie in hand.
Ignorance is so sweet...

TORN BETWEEN LOVE AND HATE

Mom, I am so tired of fighting this anger inside me...
There is now nothing that I wish for / except to just insensibly and quietly flee.
Dad, I am so tired of being always blamed for egoism...
And yes, there might be some truth to it / but it's a habit, since I'm alone in this prison.

Dears, I am so spent from all your grand expectations...
I'm begging you to give me some time / to restore my heart from your prior accusations.
Loved ones, I am exhausted of being so often misunderstood!
Yes, I might not always be rational / but I am still learning, I am still in the crude.

I beg you to finally stop expecting so much, as if it was granted!...
See, I'd be lost just for and by a little / but thanks to you, my road's gone; my freedom's branded...
I ask you to please understand: I esteem you, respect you, and owe to you;
but something must've been broken inside me long ago / is it too much to hope for some gratitude?

And yes, you might be justified, even allowed to want from me so much;
yet I'm asking you to please accept the fact / that I'm a selfish loner, always been and will be such.
And still to you, I'm grateful for all the past, for what I am and have.
I am just asking you to please forgive me / for vexing you, and being mad, and missing the enough.
I beg you to give me some time to find strength to rise after another fall...
I am still mad at you for demanding so much / my rage at me for my rage at you I can't control.

Ah, but what a dreadful fury - if held back a little, it yields a flaming pain...
I have no right to be angry with you and yet I am – for that myself can only be disdained.
For you I hate myself! And I am mad at you for this self-hate!
Yet in my turn, I've caused you trouble... hurt... / I need to reason through and let off all the bate...

Ah, I am so tired to keep this mess in mind all the time,
and through weak attempts at self-deception / convince myself of innocence of my own crime...
At guilt, at fault, to blame - I don't deserve you – it is true.
Forgive me, ungrateful, hateful... 'Cause you I've always loved... and always will... and always do.

PRETENSION GAMES

You see just what you wish to see,
and what you wish to see I see;
you play pretension games with me,
so guilty I feel not with you pretending...

...You give directions then claim it was a test,
my failure of which to not reveal I'm pressed;
so, instead, pieces of truth supplying,
I watch them forced into a puzzle
of reality you use to dazzle,
its fictitiousness denying -
the very crude puzzle that they were
never meant to be a part of.

...But you think manipulations of this kind
to be beneath my skill/ambition/mind,
as, in your eyes, I am inferior
by the mere factor of your own
perceived transcendence in flesh 'nd bone,
you feel supreme, superior,
(yet handicapped with foul impotence
to see that the alleged weak have strength).

...So I let you believe this puzzle of truth -
your genius creation or just a silly ruse -
in your reality it has no fit,
shining doubt on your view of me;
so you come back with more study,
certain that this time I'll be at a loss -
oh, how you love to degrade my worth!
(though not much is left beyond a naught.)

...And no, I'm not bright enough to see the hook,
or remember that the very same one took
my dignity already time ago;
so all I can and do, of course -
undermine those designs of yours,
giving your plans a nonfatal blow;

but I wonder if your schemes breaking,
another course of yours I'm taking,
for there is no trap as cunning as the one
that makes you think there's a trap,
when there is none.

...Yet even when you don't get what you expect,
when your directions are slighted with neglect,
you still claim triumph, your cards revealing,
which I then use to fake as mine,
armed with truth that you designed -
your scheme foreseen I'm stealing;
and for you I even provide escape,
when my theft you discover late.

...So now, my not following your directions,
and my queer answers to your questions,
are nothing more than just a chess check;
when actually I falter blind,
lost for the ways not yet designed,
but which you would expect of my
following your directions
or my refusal to follow them...

...You see just what you wish to see,
and what you wish to see I see;
you play pretension games with me,
so guilty I feel not with you pretending.

MAYBE

Maybe, oh just maybe,
sometimes laughter isn't proper,
as what's presented as a joke
is desperation crying for support,
disguised in shameful hurry;

external validation isn't cure
for damaged self-esteem;
still, it's a temporary treatment
that allows to make steps
in directions that feel right;

it feels dissonant to be refusing
to judge those that judge you,
while feeling inadequate
and deprecated
by their judgment;

if you're going to hurt me,
then have the decency and courage
to not pretend to be my friend
and mar the concept of my friendships
with your carefree betrayal,
which I can't even call "betrayal",
since the joke is on me
for allowing it to happen,
and has been all along.

Because if you try hard enough, you can break the invulnerable
and if you push long enough, you can make the strong cry;
because even the kindest might one day discover that
having poured their grace on everyone
left them empty and dry.

SELF-DECEPTION

"You lie to yourself, then blame me for hurt;
you look at my words through distorted glass.
you see what you want, and take stars for dirt,
afraid to step outside the bonds of your trust."

"I lie to myself, then blame you for ache;
I take dirt for stars - self-deception is my game.
I provide you with glass then send it to break.
We play mentally unstable while completely sane."

No need to be sorry, you say,
then add that you were free to choose -
avoid the throbs and just walk away,
or stay and watch all hell break loose.
No need to be sorry, you whisper,
then smile painfully with a side of your lip.
And I so hate to be your heart's blister -
confused of what I want,
I still burn you with my tight grip.

"I live in forced patterns, you see them for truth;
but my expectations should not even exist."

"We use self-deception as the best means of soothe,
we lie hard but get punished with just a slap on the wrist."

"You evade my forced patterns but fall prey to the game."

"I don't play with intent, yet I'm selfish to cease."

"Of us neither one is guilty, but both are to blame..."

"With truth yet to be uncovered, self-deception is our peace."

NO ONE

Erase all true emotion from your face and frame;
only say what they want to hear;
make sure to complain when they complain;
only laugh when they do; they don't feel real,
yet compared to the fake you are,
they are the realest thing in your life by far;

so, empty your mind,
then find comfort in the confines
of the box you've settled in -

become no one.

GOOD DAYS

Good days were few but costly, each costing a fortune measured in buckets of salt from my tears flavored by despair; each costing a fortune hidden in high voltage treasure vaults, filled with muted screams, electrified by hollow.

Good days were when my mind was silent of the dark and bitter future it had envisioned for me, grounded in the naive present, insulated by hope. So it became a rule during my good days to do as much of everything as I could - generating extra energy to store for later, always forgetting that accumulators fail from excessive pre-charges.

Good days were when I created the most - before the final plunge into my darkness or right after I got through the worst of it - 'cause those would still count as good days even as they electrocuted me and tasted anguish - yes, all that, but still good.

Good days were never fully free of darkness, yet mere flickers of light made them good; and each time the flickers went out, good days were paused like a jukebox, greedy for more coin.

Darkness was the apathy, low on Amperes, even lower or Watts, a complete lack of desires arisen from perceived vainness of any and all efforts; the imbalance between my negative and positive charges that would lead to static electricity on my surface - ungrounded, a danger to everyone around. In that darkness, I was a non-rechargeable battery exhausted long before its scheduled replacement time, occupying a space that'd be better served, if filled by someone else.

Darkness was the impotence to do a single thing that could be viewed as living or to even hope for a brighter future, wondering if this power outage would turn into a full scale blackout. It was the time filled with staring at blank spaces with vacant hands and idle mind, only remembering the time when I still created... wanted to create...

Darkness was the debilitation nurtured by abundance of despise for my weakness, but despise that would fail to spark an impulse or find outlet in rage or action - like using rubber as a conductor and wondering why it wasn't working. A cable wishing for a current, wanting to want, wanting to quit, then quitting to want, to wish, to even think - a failed fuse.

Darkness, bound to me by the negative potential energy, was the diminished feeling, reduced emotional response, referred with needless fancy to as hypothymia; it was the lowered consciousness degree, referred with aimless fancy to as lethargy; and darkness was so many things, but fancy it was not.

Darkness, in the very end, was just a recurring short-circuit: the ever fraying insulation of my memories of good days, with their evidence to the cursory finality of darkness, and the bared wire of my absent interest to contemplate a chance of a more vigorous life. After all, the me in darkness knew not the me of my good days, yet docilely, it always paid the price of those days.

Ilana Kovalle: Ode to Hope and Despair

All the things I am not,
all the things I will never be,
all that stings now like salt
on the wounded pride deep in me;
all the things I am not,
all the things I have failed to be,
all I thought I forgot
still claws at the wistful heart in me...

I broke myself time after time
trying to fit in the puzzle I made up.

48

WEIGHT OF DISAPPOINTMENT

so i keep on messing up, keep on doing it all wrong -
i go on when i should stop, and don't continue when alone;

i'm so sick of what i am, i'm sick of all the things i say,
thoughts in my mind, things i do, the way i act and live my day;

unworthy of a kind word, i'm such a weakling in disguise,
and when nobody is around, myself i openly despise;

i burden you i know that - i'm burdened by my own self;
to disappear i would love, but something stops me in the end;

i want to be so very strong and carry all your griefs away;
but all i am is simply wrong - my whole existence a mistake;

and strong is what i try to be, for weakness i can't help but scorn;
yet boomerang hit hard at me - i'm weak and frightful and still wrong;

your hand you offered being kind - i got to maim your whole arm;
i'm very sorry, and i'm trying to fix it all but do more harm;

i wish i could just disappear and know you've forgotten me
and all the stupid things and fears i did, said, felt, and let you glimpse;

and this is why i try to stay so far away from all around -
it's easier to bluff my way, when my bluff cannot be found;

an ugly person, that i am, but i can deal with truth alone,
for when with others, i just slip, then need by them to be condoned;

there is so much i wish to change, but i'm as useless as they come;
when you don't know me, i'm strange, but better that than vile 'n dumb;

so ignorant, so clueless too, so selfish, weak, and immature;
i am forever my own doom - self-hate's become my ax and cure.

WHAT USE

What use is there for me? What use, oh God, please tell me.
What use i have to be so far from whom i wished to be...

Oh God, if you hear me, please say that i'm in your plans,
that life will have some meaning, that i'll wake up from my trance.

What use? Should there be one? Might one be tortured vainly?
If life needn't mean a thing, why even should one keep it?

No use... no use... no use... What use to be so useless?...

So when they say that meaning is inside, and we should always turn inwards to discover it,
i look in puzzlement, wondering how there could be anything in that dead vacuum of my interior.

And when i stare inwards, as they urge me, the vacuum, its fat nothingness, stares back, its meaning in being meaningless - its whole purpose is to find the meaning in merely existing, free of pangs of doubt and regret.

And that nothingness is so ebony and thick that i can use it as ink, write its cold essence out, let it spill onto the paper, let the paper absorb that darkness and give it a form - cloak the hollow into intricate shapes of essential words, draw it out of myself;

Soon enough i watch the void, the very epiphanal lack of meaning, turn into something meaningful in and of itself - the paper, the ink - they're real, even if i still can't fathom that elusive meaning inside of me.

What if meaning is inherent and can't be created or destroyed?
What if it's not me chasing it, but it trying to claim dodgy me?
What if instead of finding it, I just need to acknowledge and welcome it?

SPRING THIS YEAR

Spring this year - some say it's having a hard time waking up;
some say it's being lazy, dumb, and slow, and should just go end itself.
But can't you see? Spring's been fighting for its very life - each move, each blink;
it's been dying, and everyone thinks it's just kidding;
it's been struggling for breath, and everyone just blames it for being weak.
Spring this year... March felt so lonely, like it had no hope to survive;
March felt like cold feet welcoming death -
not warning of it because warning is useless, but acknowledging its imminent presence,
with the cold moving up - to legs, to chest - displacing hope on its way -
sinking ice that fails to break, as it crushes on the fish, and trapped they die.
April showed then some bashful signs of life:
a patient waking from a coma, trying to move a finger here, a toe there,
through phantom flashes of green - a bud, a sprout -
confused and doubtful about its chances, still overwhelmed with weakness
that manifested in persistent attacks of white - some snow, some ice.
May... I don't know about May - it's yet to come;
I guess soon enough we'll all know if the patient improves,
but for now, let's say "Get better!" in place of "What's wrong with you?"
Sometimes a little care can go a long way...
...Spring this year - May turned out to be another wretched patient,
who had been sentenced with cancer then cured,
thrown off a cliff with a relapse then cured again,
but now cognizant of the uncertainty of the cure, its temporariness,
it tries to make up for the time lost already to the sickness
and for the time it might still lose to it by going full out - each drop, each bloom -
exhausting itself to prove something to the disease now posing a constant threat in its mind.
May tries so hard to prove itself that it has lost its very self in the process:
maniacally shifting between bursts of June and episodes of April -
unable to be itself, scared to be itself; yet despite all of that,
there's hopefulness around May -
being overly aware of the finality of the time it has,
it strives to accumulate as much happiness as it can,
even if that straining effort might end up bringing a sooner end to it.
Can't you see? Spring this year - some say it's showing strength in the face of adversity;
some say it's inspiring in its persistence - it's so lovely and should never end.

WANT

i   don't   want to be here

i   want   to be nowhere

i   don't   even care

that i   don't   want to be

yet when i say

that it hurts

to not want to live,

i'm not saying

that i

wish

to die -

no, i

do not

want

to die;

i just want

to want

to live...

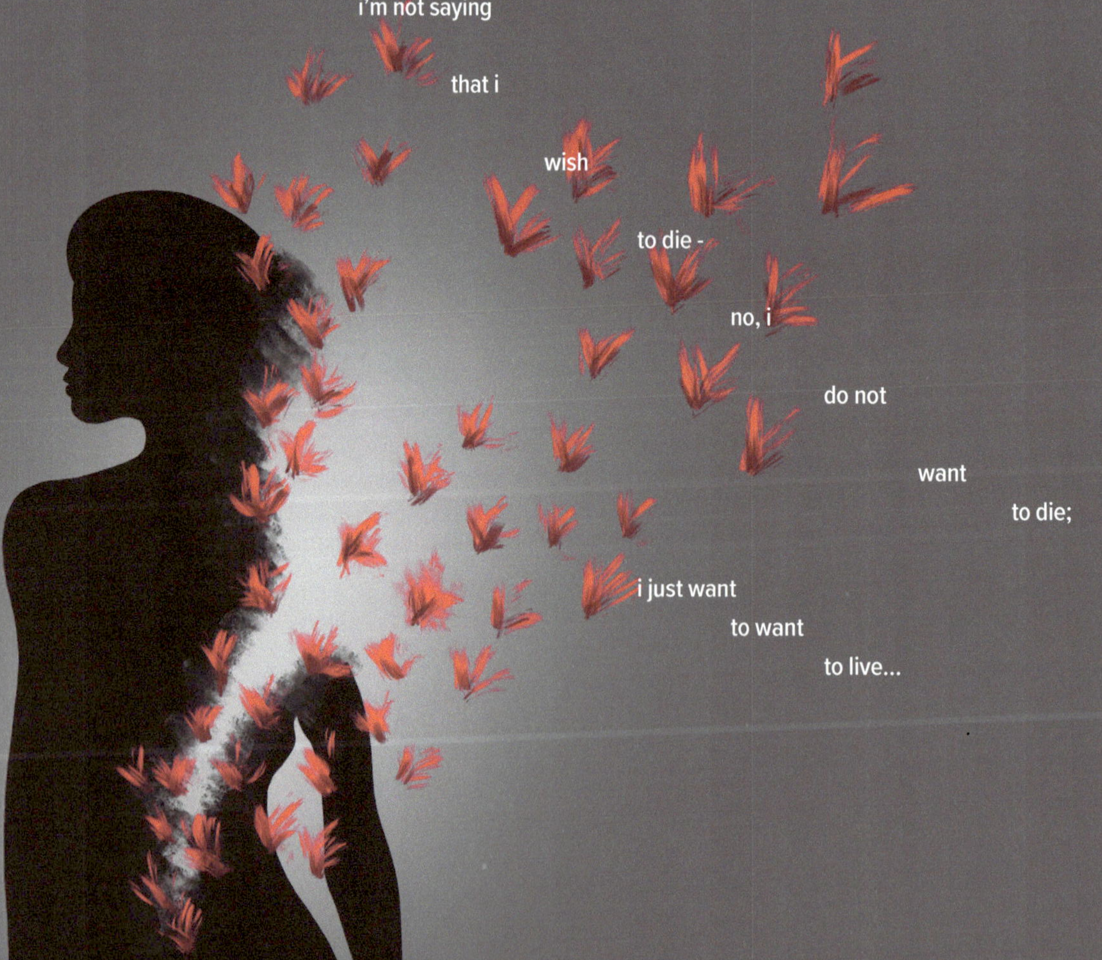

HOLLOW

Hollow inside, i'm so hollow inside.
        Black colors all around, and the sky appears grey.
            And all i want is just to be by someone's side -
                i am longing for a purpose
                    'cause its absence causes pain.

And i know people love me, i know life is good,
        but somehow, despite this knowledge, i am lost, and all's in vain.
            Living life through others' feelings - regret's my forever mood...
                Now i'm spreading out the darkness;
                  hopeless, i've missed my train.

Faking outside, always faking outside,
        i am never fully honest with myself or those around.
            All i do is just rarely trust and often hide,
                yet putting up an image of a
                  strong girl who's whole and sound.

In a conscious state of darkness, of depression conscious state,
        i am spending my whole lifetime, full aware of all the twists.
            Happiness exhausts me, while misery feels great.
                They say i can choose and i can change -
                some day, i'll tame my inner beasts.

Hollow inside, so hollow inside,
gray colors all around, and the fire appears gray;
but in the middle of that grayness, in the heart of that fire,
there's a burning-red life and hot fuel for that flame...

But what if I'm an acoustic guitar,
and the hollowness at my core
is for my soul to have the freedom to resonate?
I spent so much time and effort trying to fill in
every empty cavity I have within
that I forgot how that hollowness,
that emptiness, provides room for being.
It's not emptiness - it's just space.
Space that can but doesn't need to be occupied.
Space that is there to provide freedom
to create, to express, to feel.
Freedom to be.

WORDS OF HURT

Everybody shares what they have -
you will offer dirt if all you've got is dirt.
If the words of love come from love,
then the words of hurt must come from hurt.

When everybody tries to take away your
reason to thrive - why do you let them?
And yes it's so much harder and worse
when your own mind is siding with them...

When someone tries to throw all their hurt on you,
you can still choose whether to let it hit you;
Imagine before you the strongest of shields
that don't just deflect but absorbs all and heals you.

So I'll cut open my chest,
break my ribs and take out
that which makes and breaks my rest,
when it drowns in salty drought
of my tears; so I wrap my hands
round the heart that likes to hurt
I wash it in muddy salty streams -
sometimes cleansing comes from dirt.

...healing is a hurt transformed....

STRENGTH, A MATTER OF DEFINITIONS

> *...In the end, there was so much strength in the way*
> *she accepted her weakness and wore her vulnerability.*

I

I knew I wasn't the strongest person I'd known, but still I called myself that;
strength becoming an obsession - a wind with which my self-worth was eroding,
a wind of which I could almost blow plenty, still ignorant of the butterfly effect.
You see, strength became the language of my hypocrisy,
the bolts of judgments I thought I was not discharging,
like when I called you weak, in accusation,
for you were supposed to be mountain-firm,
enough for me to rely on your strength instead of my own;
like when I called you weaker than me, in frustration,
for by the virtue of my definitions,
I was the sturdy one and that I couldn't oversee.
You had once asked, "Where did strength bed out?"
To which I answered simply - in the power of will
to drag yourself out of bed at 5am to work for your heart's dreams
before punching in the hours for your stomach's needs;
to push yourself to taking action instead of loathing your body
and letting the landslide of your sloth eat at the baby roots of strength.

II

I knew I didn't have the right to call me strong, for I'd been fortunate to have avoided most scourges,
which would have annealed me at the cost I would have never paid of my free will;
a few calamities of life couldn't turn me into a martyr. But did strong ones never break
or were they strong because they had reforged their once fractured pieces?
You see, when strength is shared, one only needs be strong by half,
but with you I felt I had to be strong by two - strong for the both -
a mountain next to a boulder, and I was so tired of being made of stone -
a boulder pretending to be a mountain;
and I'd been thus strong until I no longer was - a silly boulder swallowed by an avalanche,
a slide of the revolting taste of that, which I'd despised in others,
and weak I toppled in my karmic fall;
I still knew how to be strong for others' sake, just not my own.
You had once asked, "Where did strength bud out?"
To which I answered simply - in the love for life;
that ability to rebuild the ruptured city of your inner peace
and move on despite the aftershocks;
to forgive the ground for its shaking or seek a firmer ground;
to waive all rights to complaints and excuses,
if you choose to do nothing to change the state of your world.

III

I knew I was far from having the strength to be proud of, as I turned into a bully,

whose strength required denial thereof in others; and each time I called you weak was a punch

that landed on you violently, for how dared you seem fragile and be ignorant of it;

yet there was nothing you could do about that, powerless,

you had no control over my definitions of strength, or how you weren't fitting them.

> You see, you made it glacier-clear though, when we last talked,
>
> that this whole time you thought me weak;
>
> you didn't hold disgust for weakness the way I did,
>
> but you still stormed that I had dared to claim to be more tough than you -
>
> your definition of strength rather different from my own -
>
> oblivious of the fact that you were the movement of tectonic plates
>
> that brought up the worst, the weakest, the wickedest in me.
>
> > You had once asked, "Where did strength bloom?"
> >
> > To which I answered simply - in the wisdom
> >
> > to know when to appear strong for another's sake
> >
> > and not tell someone who had been ravaged by a tsunami of your venom,
> >
> > about how much you might feel torn apart yourself, a whisperer of waves;
> >
> > and not talk of how in a fire, one is more likely to die of suffocation than of burns,
> >
> > and so you can't help but contemplate your gas stove as a means to a smoky end,
> >
> > a manipulator dressed as a victim.

IV

I knew I wasn't the strongest person there was, but still I chose to believe I could be:

strength - a matter of definitions, a meaning that seemed obvious and universal,

a meaning I thought could not be misunderstood,

unaware of our tendency to overestimate how clear we come across,

like waves that shimmer pure in the sun above their muddy bodies.

> You see, I had succumbed to weakness before I met you;
>
> yet as feeble as I was, I still saw myself more sound than you:
>
> one - a boulder feigning to be a mountain, another - a pebble believing to be a boulder;
>
> I just didn't expect your weakness would be the collapse of my strength,
>
> setting me on a path of annealing that I never desired
>
> to pay the price of until I had no choice,
>
> a boulder turned out to be an eggshell.
>
> > So, was I strong, when in my weakness,
> >
> > I still could feel the soft concern of raindrops?
> >
> > Was I strong, when in my numbness, I still enjoyed the scent of lilacs,
> >
> > despite the knowledge they were your flower of choice?
> >
> > Was I strong, when in my darkness, I heard the cheer of first snow flurries?
> >
> > Was I strong, when in my torment, I learned to laugh
> >
> > again?

MY GOD

Last night I talked to God, and it said I'd be okay;
I asked to help me make a choice, and it said
I already had all the answers I needed inside of me.

Where is this God of mine, you ask?

I'm not sure how to explain, but let me try. That absent feeling of loneliness when I'm alone - that's where God's present. It's the tickling reminder of a world within me. God tickles, did you know? It's in me, it's around me, it's everywhere and nowhere at the same time. I don't always remind myself to focus on its presence, just as I don't always remind myself to breathe, but still notice when I don't or can't. Similarly, I notice when God gets further away, or rather, when I get further away from it - when I let the world grow *between* us, instead of *within* us; when I become its part, without first becoming my whole.

For me, there's no religion, and God doesn't have an objective to watch me or judge me or take care of me. It's just a bundle of energy, a higher power that is simply there, just like I am simply here. Still, if it doesn't have intentions, then I can assign it any intentions of my liking, and so I let it be caring. And I don't know, maybe for other people it's done true miracles or maybe they were coincidental and attributed to it by mistake, but for me, God is a source of nonloneliness. So no, I can't say I know God is there, but I do feel its presence, and I choose to interpret that presence as benevolent.

But if we create God in our image,
does that mean that my source of nonlonliness is myself?

MISS YOU

You know, I already miss you -
miss the way you'd finish my phrases,
knowingly glimpse at me sideways,
and we would then burst out laughing.

Hey, you know, I really miss you -
miss the frail mentions of our pasts
as we'd confide in one another,
trust being something we both long craved.

You know, I'm here, I still miss you...
Miss how you'd thaw my loneliness
in the sea of care and shared dreams;
similar, we grew together.

You know, I miss you.
Miss our strong, yet subtle, sense of safeness,
as I'd unwrap my bandaged soul,
and trusting you would bare yours.

You know, I'll soon cease to miss you -
miss the feeling of belonging
that you used to let me bask in,
and I hope I gave that to you.

You know, I almost don't miss you -
that's what I still tell myself,
as I try, want, to be happy
that you found somebody better.

You know, I no longer miss you -
that's what I'd like to say one day,
but for now, I just try so hard
to not resent that you left me behind.

ATTENTION SEEKER

Relief was a cold shower, when i realized i hurt myself or seek danger
not only for my partiality to the adrenaline spice in my mouth
each time i bite on my lip in the process, and not only for the safety from the madness that ensues,
when my mind's ache isn't matched by my body's suffering, but also to quench
my inner child's thirst for care - broken bones tasted better when served in mom's broth,
and nosebleeds splashed parental attention into the monochrome of a self-sufficient kid.

So my health i neglect, aggravate it with risk-seeking behavior -
so craving love and care from others, that i undermine my love and care for my own self;
so hungry for any notice from others that i engage in intentional starvation -
the less there is of me, the more they pay attention;
it's never been an active thought or open intent but looking back now, i see it's been there all along:
when i almost scored sepsis by neglecting my swollen arm, even as it didn't fit in any sleeves,
when i strained my ligament yet persisted till i tore it up completely;
when i allowed myself no proper sleep or food, taking grim satisfaction in being purposefully weak,;
when i stood too close to the platform edge - train approaching, eyes closed, swinging hopefully;
or when i rollerbladed on highways at night, all clad in black that screamed to cars "please, hit me."

There, you have the truth now - i'm a little sulking whiny
seeker of attention, a child thirsty for affection, but using
all the wrong ways to try to come by it.

...they say you cut yourself to seek attention,
and you should be ashamed of that,
but they don't even stop to ponder
that seeking attention through hurting yourself
should imply anything but shame:
it's a cry for help that whispers timidly
in the face of implicit hostility towards its mere nature,
and in whisper it says that for some reason,
it feels right to have to pay for attention and care
with pain and hurt and ache and suffering.
i don't cut my wrists or ankles,
but i learned that i don't need a razor
to engage in self-harm...

WRITING A LOVE LETTER TO MYSELF

"a love letter to myself"

i pause at the title for a few minutes
or maybe a few hours, finally deciding to

let it steep for a day, hoping it'll brew into a reviving potion
that will satisfy the thirst for that title to be more than a title,

in the way that chewing a rubber gum of falsehood refuses to;
there are few times when i hungered more for the truth

to have the same flavor as the lie
than when i was trying to sanction the recipe for self-love;

let it sit for two days, hoping it'll enter the effervescence phase
and oxidize into a divine elixir that would claim my sobriety, swat me into inebriation,

and color all ugly stains of abstinence with a virgin's blood;
there are few times when i regretted

the absence of substance in my veins more
than when trying to find words of love for myself;

let it be for three days, hoping it would grow mold,
the penicillin kind, a fairy pollen to disinfect my mind's wounds, bloom into poppies,

and whither into morphine to calm the sting of the disinfection;
there are few times i loved myself less

than when trying to write a love letter to myself.

Each "I love you" is a stab to my esteem
that believes so sacredly that it could never be worthy of that love.
Any love.

For shouldn't love signify a beginning?
How could it possibly exist next to the continuous struggle for an end?

It's easy to love when loving is easy, but what if love truly counts when you love through the hard?

ROPES

You're twisting my words
into ropes you use
to tie up my hands
to toss on my neck;

You're finding things
in your memory's attic
that I don't recall but
you never forgot;

Your hands full of stones
you've carried with you
across all these years,
waiting for when you
would get to use them
against me;

Confused
you are now,
for they've grown roots,
weighing you down
refusing to leave you,
as easy as when
you once left me.

THERE WAS A TIME

There was a time, when the girl was fearless.
 Sure, she was still afraid of that moment in the shower,
 when she needed to close her eyes while washing her head,
 or the rhythmic creaks in her empty house that were loudest at night,
 but those she didn't count as fears that precluded one from being fearless;
 though she also didn't know there were other things for her to fear -
 like waking up and wishing hard to hear those rhythmic creaks
 over a stranger's breath in her ear, or learning that the stranger was a friend -
 and so she was fearless in her ignorance;
 for it's easy to not fear that, which you don't know yet to fear.

There was a time, when the girl didn't know doubt.
 Uncertainty was just a cloak of potential, on occasion baring a shoulder
 and offering chances, each "not sure" filled with surprises,
 before she learned to hate surprises,
 before uncertainty pulled the cloak over its head to reveal an executioner's hood
 and tore to shreds her peace of mind,
 turning her into a stupefied puppet that couldn't act even when prompted to.

And there was a time, when the girl
 knew not there was something that she wasn't capable of,
 knew not she wasn't good enough to try and strive and dream and fight,
 when she still had no idea that her struggles
 were impossibilities, thinking them mere obstacles to overcome,
 obstacles whose existence didn't define her as inherently deficient;
 knew not that fighting those struggles was to be her road with no destination,
 knew not that she'd box herself in a belief that she had to be boxed in,
 or that happiness was in being unaware that she didn't have that which she didn't have.
 It might be ignorance, but for the ignorant it was a mercy she was jealous of.

There was a time when the girl lived
with the knowledge of finality of happiness,
and that knowledge gave rise to despair;
there was a time when the girl lived
with the knowledge of finality of misery,
and that knowledge gave birth to hope.

HFD

High-functioning depression is a depression infested with anxiety:

I once turned worries into mosquitos and swatted and plucked them out of my hair,
but they laid eggs, and their larvae mutated into something else -
now it's anxious thoughts irrupting as one tight roach cloud,
so tight that I can't pick a single insect apart
from the giant body they merged into,
infiltrating each crevice of my cortex,
crawling out of the bunkers of each gyrus,
which are supposed to be my safe places,
reducing safety to the instants between
the scratches of their sticky legs on my meninges.

insufficient

behind

unworthy

unlovable

waste

...I wish I didn't know each crawler by its name -
somehow that makes it harder to exterminate them...

SOMETIMES

Sometimes the world feels so hopeless
that we lose faith in people,
not because they betray us,
but because they betray themselves.

Sometimes the world looks so beautiful
that it hurts to see the contrast
between our little deformed selves
and everything around.

Sometimes we can't reach out for help
'cause then we would need to admit
that we failed at our attempt
to be the source of help for others.

Sometimes...
We tend to fall without light;
we tend to fall with no support;
surrender's our first resort -
we tend to give up on the fight.

Sometimes...
In misery we tend to sulk
about how life's unfair,
yet make a change we don't dare,
and misery is left to bulk.

Sometimes...
When we don't do the right things,
we cannot do things right;
of what's important we lose sight -
and crawl around with broken wings.

Sometimes...
By seeking to be better than someone,
we end up worse than ourselves.

PATTERN-BOUND

When you feel underserving of your yet unborn children;
when you feel like a burden to your yet unmet partner;

when you learn you've been stomping
on the same spot for years -
the same old spot to which you always return;

no matter how far you manage to escape -
the escape is never for long.

So I cringe going forward - I'm stepping on needles,
I'm barefoot, and ruthless, they pierce my feet.

Each small step forward is full of throbbing fiddles;
I march on out of a habit -
meaningless habit I wish I could quit.

The farther back I look the happier I was -
didn't think of happiness, it simply was around.

Now scary milestones make me feel at a loss:
life's an illusion of choice - in the end,
we are all simply
pattern-bound.

INCOHERENT

*How I wish I could just know
how far I've travelled yet,
and how far I've yet to go,
before I am cold and dead.*

I try so hard to stop me from thinking
how utterly useless I happen to be;
yet in my darkness I keep on sinking
and watch it consume the whole of me.

I try so hard but bring no value
into the world and to those around;
one question hammers me - "Really, shall you
continue to struggle if you've already drowned?"

So
I grind my teeth, refusing to cry,
denying that something is very wrong;
the easiest tactic that works - to deny,
go numb 'n blind and pretend to be strong.

And I try so hard to not be angry
that I have got nothing to offer of use,
that instead of fighting I think of ending,
and tie the knot on my own noose.

Just twenty something, yet I feel old and tired -
so empty and heavy, so numb and confused;
maybe that's how my brain is wired,
but no - it's all yet another excuse.

I wish to be big and I wish to be strong,
be warm and bright and have value inherent;
but all that I am and have been is alone,
weak, little, and small, and quite incoherent.

SOLITUDE vs. LONELINESS

Solitude is often seen as a punishment, but the first thing it is is a choice. Solitude is not a diagnosis that requires treatment; rather it's a preferred condition of the soul. Solitude is not something we inflict upon ourselves for being different; rather it's freedom bestowed on us for having the senses, the aptitude to learn and benefit from it. Solitude is not something to fear or hate; it's something to desire for understanding and achieving completeness of our existence. Solitude is no punishment - it's a blessing in disguise.
If only solitude was what I had...

Up till now I have lived with shades over my eyes,
as if this whole time I've grieved all my unattempted tries;
and these shades hid so well the world's true shapes and hues -
green squares taken for red circles, a lie I've taken for a truth:
I thought that I was self-sufficient,
when all I ever really was
was lonely.

I don't say I'm lonely though - busy is a much nicer word to use. So, when I say I'm really busy, I mean that I'll find plenty of stuff to stay late at work for, just to avoid going home, where nobody's waiting. When I say I'm busy, I mean that I'm planning to spend hours choosing a movie to watch, only to fall asleep a few minutes into it. I'm busy means I feel anxious when I have free time because that free time is where phantom laughter of my likely-to-never-be-born children lives.

...The emptiness in my heart is a habitual feeling
the bothering buzzing of which I often seek to smother with idly busy bustle,
while the mind flips through the memories of people
who could've absorbed that emptiness with their presence,
if only I'd let them...

WISH (reprise)

I wish I would just disappear
and leave no trace of having been,
no unnecessary tears
and aches to those
loving me.

"I wish I would just disappear" -
six tiny words, one single phrase -
how can it drag year after year?
How can words hurt
more than a blaze?

I wish I would just disappear.
A feeling cloaked into thoughts -
my coy escape from reeling fears
that what's ahead
is somehow worse:

not that in the future I still hurt,
but that my hurt's still all I see.

CURSE

And maybe the curse is not to not be good at anything,
but rather to have no interest in pursuing that which you're good at;
desiring instead to do that for which you have no natural aptitude,
hitting your head against the ceiling of glass that you created yourself.

It was the easiest thing to say that she didn't have what it takes:
that she was born without the talent to do the things she wanted to do -
        a penguin staring wistfully at the sky above;
that the universe decided to be ironic and play a joke on her,
        giving her the desire but not the skills;
that the universe was cruel, as it promised her wings
        but never mentioned that she was to be born an earthbound cassowary;
that she wasn't lucky enough to have others' help and guidance,
        a flightless Campbell teal amongst wild ducks.
It was easy to say that she was tired of swimming against the current, of fighting.

It wasn't just the talent that she lacked though
        - hard work can make up for talent absent in more cases than not -
it was the inner drive:
        she was always a chrysalis, never a butterfly;
forever stuck in her transformation, lost for direction, not knowing which way was out;
        a gosling trapped under a layer of ice,
thin enough to tease with the proximity of freedom but not enough to let escape.
        She was dramatic in her misery too.

She saw her depression as another show of her weakness -
        it was much easier to wish to not exist, to unexist,
than to continue fighting against the odds.
        And she regularly pleaded guilty to succumbing to those easy ways.

She saw the world for what it wasn't,
        and her dreams for what they couldn't be.
She picked the wrong element, then focused on breaking herself to fit within its confines.
        She was still ignorant of how stubborn penguins tamed water for their dreams
and learned to fly in their own way.

A PERSON UNCOMMON

A person uncommon -
who doesn't fit in,
who refuses to trade
acceptance for freedom.

A person of courage
isn't foreign to fear
and finds the strength
in protecting the weaker.

A person of goodness
has and been wronged,
knows vices in person,
yet is kind by choice.

A person of morals
isn't blindly lawful
and knows to question
standard norms and beliefs.

A person uncommon -
the one you look up to,
the one you could be too,
if you weren't afraid.

COLOR OF SILENCE

The drawing was quiet:
as quiet as a silence saturated with screams;
as quiet as a heart without hope;
as quiet as the world that lost its ability to hear,
overwhelmed by the cries for help;
as quiet as a drawing should be.

Lines and angles scattered
like dismembered words;
its colors attempting to build a muddy rainbow;
the drawing was supposed to mean something,
and it probably did, she just couldn't read it yet,
for it was drafted in a language
she had forced herself to unremember.

Drawing was part of her therapy,
but she was rather terrible at it,
equally terrible at both, or maybe
she was only terrible at one thing -
that of getting better.

The pencil between her fingers felt soft;
almost as soft as her tongue had felt,
when it had failed to obey her,
when it remained silent -
too soft to succeed at conveying the horror
inside her mind
to the outer world.

She turned the page and stared
at the whiteness of its other side -
the terrain of possibilities,
the blank slate that could become
anything she chose.

She let the pencil dive headfirst
into the middle of the sea of white -
all there was in front of her now
was a black dot;
a single black dot that had the power
to erase the possibilities
that existed before it.

A single black dot that became
her point of partial singularity,
where the past, the present,
and the future merged in a way
that wouldn't let her escape any of them:
Was her present her future?
Did she still live in her past?
But if her future was her present,
was her past her future then?
Was it all inevitable?

Wherever she shifted her gaze,
it always returned to that single black dot
that commanded her attention in a way
the possibilities around it no longer could;
wherever she shifted her gaze,
the black dot went with it,
projecting itself onto everything else,
dying the blank slate of her
unremembering mind
into the color of blood of a rainbow smashed -
the color of silence.

*...Just uncovered another layer of scar tissue -
didn't realize how deep was the cut.*

WORDS

Words are escaping my mind,
like fireflies teasing the blind,
like butterflies flying too high,
with windmill hands, in vain I try.

Thoughts are betraying my trust,
like sturdy iron turned to rust,
like fake stars that are long gone,
in charge before, now I'm a pawn.

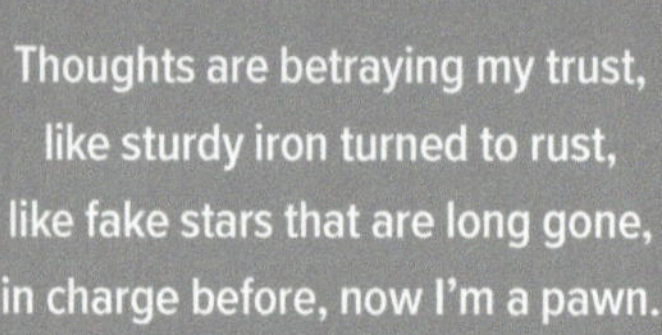

The more I look for words to describe
that barren feeling residing inside,
the farther I feel those words escape -
emptiness inside forming its own shape.

*Last night was one
of those sleepless nights,
full of raucous poignancy
of a beehive
swarming in my thoughts;*

*With the mind
being a child
that froze in the midst of it all,
lost as to what
it should do next;*

*...But now
the bees are gone,
the child moved on.*

PET BEAST

I have an excuse that I cannot use:
it pulls at my hand, holds down my mind,
shackles me home, away from the others,
who justly resent me for another flake-out -
the excuse would be an insult,
so I don't offer it.

I have a pet beast that robs me of peace:
it claws at me for things it forgives
to others; it holds all in double standards,
where I'm always on the losing side;
like a cat with a caught mouse,
my pet beast doesn't realize -
its games can lead to my demise.

Yes, my pet beast's to blame as it isn't quite tamed:
it tends to exist in a shape of a hamster,
an innocent whisper that couldn't cause harm,
till relaxed and trusting, I close my eyes,
and it grows in size and heightens in temper -
the whisper is now a yell, sharp teeth of which
grind at my will.

I have an excuse that I cannot use:
I cling on to it, as it clings on to me,
we're co-dependent for survival,
parasitic life, in which we ruin each other -
it can ease my misery,
but it's also its
cause.

...For the longest time I thought I was struggling to tame the little spoiled brat of a hamster that was compromising my thoughts, but it turned out I was the hamster, doing all that compromising.

WORST ENEMY

I simply stood right there,
so stuck in my own head,
terrified that I had dared
to even try to run ahead.
In this game that had been fixed
against me right from the start,
I was forced to play a role -
a little silly preset part.

So I simply stood right there,
in my nerves and doubts stewed;
their question in the air
"Why, at all, should we choose you?"
And I felt so undeserving -
a fake, impostor - can't they see?!
For my very worst opponent
was no other one than... me.

In my mind I know perfection
can never truly be achieved;
yet each error and rejection
eat at the core of my esteem.
You don't need to say a word,
don't even need to hold a grudge:
I'll beat me up of my own accord -
I'm my own hangman and my judge.

The story ended long ago,
but my mind keeps on listing
all the things I should've known,
and the chances I'd been missing:
Why did I ever do that thing?
Why did I ever use that phrase?
A bee that bit her own sting;
I don't belong to any place.

In my hands, which are so frugal and tender,
I hold the power to be my worst offender;
I hold the power to cause me so much pain -
my slain heart save in vain just to destroy again.
In my hands, which are so frugal and tender,
I hold the power to be my best defender;
I hold the power to heal any of my ache -
my fake heart break at stake and all for my true self's sake.

RAIN

The rain shed the tears I couldn't.

Each drop broke into a myriad more, simultaneously a beginning and an end.

I could ignore them no more than I could ignore the value of the lives around me: they broke apart and they resurfaced in those they had broken into - each life a beginning of another, each an end in and of itself.

I stood, listening to the rain drops, allowing them to fill my mind, my consciousness.

It was all I was at that moment - rain drops - and I didn't want the moment to end.

Will you listen to the rain with me?

SPIRAL

It took her a very long time to realize that she was falling.

She looked around, where nothing seemed different - the buildings, the people, the laughter, the eyes - they were all around her, moving in customary circular notions. Yet that circle wasn't a circle - it was a spiral, and it was spiraling down, bringing her along.

It was the enormous diameter of the first few levels of the spiral that made it feel still, a snake in a hideout before an attack. And as she slowly slid down the inaudibly hissing circle of faces, believing herself to be in control, she was yet unaware that just a few levels later, the angle would steepen, and she would have lost her opportunity to jump out of the snake's mouth, before it swallowed her whole.

So now, falling she was, refusing to believe it, refusing to acknowledge it, refusing to deal with it. Couldn't she just will it out of existence? If she did nothing about it, wouldn't it just stop in futility?

She could see herself falling too. It was the strangest sensation to be an observer to the disaster enveloping her body, and not attempting, even instinctively, to do anything about it. There seemed to be some unspoken agreement of implied surrender with the brume surrounding her, the brume that was darker than the glares she shot at herself in the occasional reflections; with the emptiness that had the strongest gravitational pull on her; with the despair calling out to her from the hungriest depths of this bottomless abyss she was now impetuously descending into. It was an agreement with a cult of foes that had been her foes for so long that the certainty of their codependent coexistence burned the hairs on her skin, filling the air with a nauseating scent, which was saying that just as she couldn't get away from them, they couldn't exactly exist without her either. In a way, they needed her, and there was some perverse gratification in being needed in her most useless form.

The snake's rotting insides, taking form of her cult of foes, were all around her, and she started to dissolve into them, becoming the very snake that had gulped her down. Her feet jerked in surprise, as they finally reached the bottom, landing on the soft intestine of her foes, sinking in the tissue upon impact, only to bounce back up, to the deceitfully safe levels of the spiral.

As she cautiously ascended, she still focused on the receding darkness so much that the fear of what was to come next left her paralyzed, without the slightest hope for a possibility of a good outcome. Yet, after passing more levels of the spiral, she managed to spot reasons for that hope to resuscitate itself - light bunnies timidly tickling her every time she dared to leave

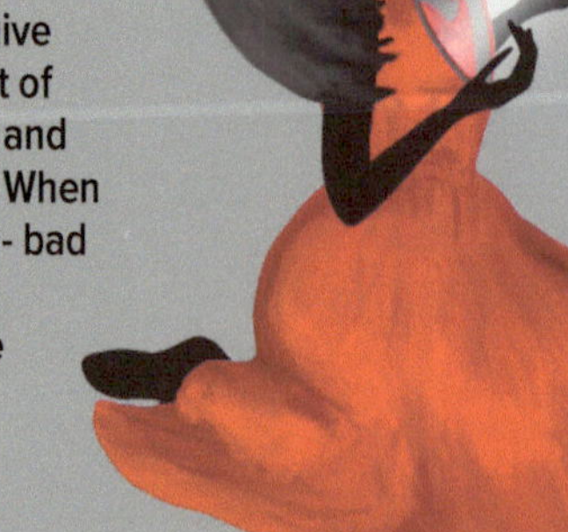

her acidic placenta of negativity and fear - a mocking souvenir from her foes, which she had gently wrapped herself in. And with those bunnies, always came a ringing reminder that it all could've been worse but wasn't because she was still able to feel the tickles and thus had another chance to turn things around, to avoid being digested.

...And after thousands of such descents and ascents, she finally learned that when darkness surrounded her in its sticky loneliness and hopelessness, it was better for her to give in and embrace it, to let herself dive deep and face the worst of the situation, as that also helped her stop fearing that worst and follow more easily the guiding beacons of her light bunnies. When everything that could go wrong did, she learned to just let it - bad things could happen without defining her or her life.

That was when her snake spirals began to become shorter and less hungry....

UNLIVING

Mud. Damp weeds
leave fingerprints
on my jeans,
as i walk through them.

Broken branches
reach out to find
in my blood
a way to heal.

Numbed marble
smolders at night,
wailing chills
down my nape.

Unliving.
Cemetery is
where my heart
belongs.

ALL THE SOUND

All the sound that remained to me was
the swish of my heart, as it dropped from its orbit;
the swish that turned to whistle, as the speed picked up,
echoing the void around it
with the void inside,
as it was falling with no direction
'cause outside its orbit there was no up or down.

As the whistle strengthened, i grew tenser,
dreading what was coming, once the fall was at its end;
the swish of the fall was a scream of despair,
but there was no sound outside of the orbit,
so the scream and the whistle were just imaginary echoes
that counted down the collision point with intensity instead of time,
collision inescapable yet unpredictable;
and the count down measured in the heart throbs since the fall began,
and not the remaining heart beats till the collision;
as the uncertainty about when that collision will occur
added to the dread inherent in the ever strengthening whistle.

All i see and feel right now
is a sting that pierces deeply,
mind that surrenders meekly,
as it cares not for later.
So please, don't tell me it'll go
'cause i know that already,
but right now, at this instant,
the future matters not.

OCTOPUS

Have you ever observed the breathing growth of a live ink cloud released by an octopus -

how it penetrates each molecule of water in its way, enswathes it from within,
acting like the octopus itself, as it devours the molecule, melding with it;

how that cloud, in its formlessness and constant movement looks so soft, so appealing to the touch, soft in the
same way that piranha's skin is, ominous and threatful in its appeal;

yet the cloud isn't ruthless in its actions - it just doesn't have control
(and it doesn't even realize it needs to have control) over its nature.

This unstoppable spread of darkness, as it envelops and turns everything else into itself is how I would
describe the impulsive action taking place in my mind upon each slight irritation of the usually dormant
octopus.

RUMBLINGS

They say I shouldn't care what others say. They say
it's wrong that I need a voice, an eye, an ear from
the outside to validate my existence. So I start
to feel ashamed and wrong about wishing to be
heard.

* * *

They say I give them power, when I ask for their
approval. But approval isn't what I'm seeking -
all I've ever asked for is to belong, to share, to
connect; and telling a story and knowing that
someone's listening is my way to feel connection.

* * *

A wise musician once said, "Singing the songs you
wrote only to yourself is like screaming into an
empty void, where even echo is absent."
I'll add that creating without sharing feels like
raising a wonderful child unseen by the world.
If everyone ignores you, how long before you start
doubting your own existence?

* * *

My art is the language I speak - and speaking can
get hard, when nobody's there to listen.After all,
the surest way to lose a language is to not use it.
So without an ear to listen, I don't speak,
and the language dies, and I go with it.

* * *

These needs - to feel heard, seen, belonging -
are basic social needs ingrained by evolution;
so why do they tell me that I claim to have less
worth, when I say it's not enough for me
to create just for myself?

* * *

I don't need their criticism, I know exactly what I'm
doing wrong. But thanks to them, I have no idea
what I'm doing right.

* * *

Everybody needs that one person who believes in
them, even when they themselves have lost
that belief.

* * *

In the depths of our fight with inner demons, the
smallest act of external support can go a long way
- *sometimes, we need to be shown that we can't
see the light not because it's dark, but because we
are it.*

* * *

I hope to have at least one person at my side, who
is glad that I exist, who sees value in my life and
can remind me of it, whenever I forget.

* * *

In the end, I want my life to have a witness outside
of me - I don't want to live an unobserved life
(I could but I don't wish to) -
and I learned there's nothing wrong with that want.

In the times of darkness,
when my mirror turns into a window
of a sunken submarine
lying in the ocean's depths,
when my senses desert me,
I need someone on the outside
to let me know I'm still here,
to see me when I can't,
and hear me when I won't.

AUTOPILOT

Most of my life
I spend on autopilot,
carelessly unaware of my days,
not registering my existence -
minty scent of the lip balm,
chipped edge of the favorite mug,
stranger's smile on the train,
laughter from an open window,
river's color at sunset,
clouds' texture at sunrise -
exposed to so much life,
yet living consciously so little,
just existing,
floating through space
as if this whole thing
is just a rehearsal
before a big debut
that never comes.

Yet well, autopilot and I -
it's complicated between us:
loss of awareness isn't always
the cost - too often, it's a gift,
a slumber, I'll pay anything to stay in.

'Cause when I wake up from it,
it's always with a gasp,
like from a dream involving free fall,
yet a free fall that doesn't end with awakening
but rather is the state after it -

the fall from a dull dream of illusions
into a swampy grayness of reality,
where I'm suspended
in between the nothingness,
where my senses betray me
refusing to give me
the flavors, the hues,
the vibrations in the air,

all gobbled up by the void of despair,
the void that I can't feel because I am it,
the void that just keeps me there wishing
to never having turned off that autopilot,
wishing to go back to the blissful state
of careless dullness;

and I'm suspended and yet I'm slipping
through the cracks,
whose edges are razor teeth,
tearing at me and shaving me apart,
and maybe I'm bleeding,
but I don't know, as I have no senses here,
I am the void,
and the razor teeth are me as well;

the free fall that I crave to end,
even if that means
smashing into the ground
and never floating again,
with or without autopilot.

INCANTATION

*read while looking in the mirror

Fear not the darkness, fear not the cold,
look into the abyss, stray from your road;

think of all the worst things that could ever occur,
survive them in our mind - acceptance is our cure;

be strict with yourself but know the limits -
no good ever comes from self-hating minutes;

learn from your mistakes, grow fond of imperfections,
easier than to hate is to express affections;

how you view the world is how it will view you too -
your attention will decide what is possible and true;

embrace your flaws and faults, reflect on shameful deeds,
life rarely ends with fulfillment of your needs;

one step at a time, there's nothing you can't do,
look deep inside your heart - inspiration's within you.

forgive yourself for errors, toss the burden of resent,
become your own most supportive and reliable friend.

PUPPET

I am just nobody,
And Nobody's my name.
You don't have to tell me -
I see it in your eyes.
But you too are nobody,
And Nobody's your name.
You're sad to see yourself in me -
Your eyes reveal that much.

She avoided eye contact.

Not because she was afraid of what she'd see in their - anyone's - eyes, but because she knew that whatever she'd see, she'd become. She was just an unwilling chameleon constantly reflecting her environment without being its real part; the strength of her mirror neurons working against her. She didn't want to find herself playing yet another role someone else had invented for her, and yet without those roles, there wasn't her - she was a bland puppet with mirrors for the eyes. If there was nothing to reflect, there really was nothing in those eyes of hers. Or was there?

She thought that her most harmful deep-set conviction was that she believed herself to be helpless, when it turned out that she actually believed herself to be worthless - so much so, that helplessness came as an obvious consequence. After all, how could she ask for help when she didn't think she had a right for it or deserved it, or that she was worthy of being helped (since she could only be worthy if she managed without it)? A contradiction? She was full of those. Or was she just afraid of owning up to being no less than those around her, that she had no less reason to be happy than they to be unhappy? Well, almost - she was afraid of needing to go ahead and accept her struggles as a normal obstacle that everyone overcame without turning it into an excuse for her littleness and nobodyness.

She also didn't like her newly found self-awareness and the awoken inner voice of conscious reflection - the two sucked all the juices out of her self-loathing, or rather her attempts at it. It suddenly occurred to her that the emotion she was feeling and being confused by wasn't even self-loathing anymore - that one she knew how to deal with (by not dealing with it) - no, it was the bizarre yearning for self-loathing, for worthlessness, and the safety net of excuses they granted. The two had been parts of her for so long - now she was a recovering alcoholic, licking her dry lips at the display of her personal vises at a friend's house. It used to feel right, deserved, to self-hate, and now, the not-hating felt wrong and out of place. There was a strange preference for certain misery over uncertain happiness - somehow, the predictability of unhappiness was alluringly comforting.

For the longest time, instead of cutting off her strings, she had desired and sought to get out of her head, flee the dungeon of her mind, escape herself and never come back. And she grew desperate after each unsuccessful attempt, not giving thought to the fact that they could never be successful, or she would not be there to announce the success. Yet the dungeon spoke back sometimes, and she realized that if anything, she was no Pinocchio inside a greedy whale - she was the whale with silly Pinocchio inside; and when her dungeon spoke, it was really her, reaching out to herself. In a terrifying growl that breathed frustration, irritation, and at the same time, compassion and care - a pet grizzly bear of a sort. And when she listened carefully, it roared in a whisper, "If you can't escape your mind, make your mind a better place, so that there'd be no need to escape it." And soon enough, she obeyed.

IRON RING

When an iron ring
tightly closed in
around my mind;
when in the mirror
I couldn't see clear
the girl I hoped to find;
when inside my heart
all I felt was a shard
of a broken dream;
I still chose to go on,
I felt weak yet was strong,
my will filling in
for my absent esteem.

When the voice inside
said that I should hide
what I really am;
when the shell they could see
was more welcome than me,
I felt like a scam;
when my hateful self
would always delve
on my smallest mistake;
I still chose to climb,
move one step at a time,
refusing to break.

Every single day,
every one of us
is fighting in a battle
that nobody sees;
so when you look around,
keep your judgments to yourself -
all lost wish to be found -
let's start by finding ourselves.

AUTUMN

Autumn has pulled its melancholy blanket over the city, wrapping everything in sumptuously sweet sadness - the nostalgia sadness, the homesickness sadness, the completion sadness.

The first is a sadness of returning to your childhood home only to realize there's nothing for you there anymore: what you feel is just love for a ghost of your past; you think you miss the place, when in reality, it's the carefree time you wish to experience again. Memories framed in gold, yet gold melting, seeping into each available crevice, revealing copper underneath. In the end, your childhood home is nothing but a pyre of crumbling leaves of copper-smudged memories throbbing with the soft pale beats of orange slices of bittersweet nostalgia - a where that's more of a when; a when that will never happen again.

Puffs of smoke in place of clouds;
dusty air shimmers in the sun; oily river's too lazy to splash,
September.

The second is a kind of sadness that overcomes you on the final night of your home visit, as you're trying to remember why it is that you can't stay; why it is that you left in the first place. And as you say goodbye, locking yourself in a wreath with your loved ones, you become the sun that their sunflowers turn to; feeling privileged to bathe in their aroma, determined to never exhale it; hoping to see them again soon enough and yet knowing that no "soon enough" is actually enough soon. Fall is when the sun beams with deception, hinting at warmth in the brightness of its light yet turning that warmth into an empty promise.

Silky lead spilled in the sky;
frigid air surprises coddled lungs; mercury nurses unbared shore;
October.

The third is a sadness that's hard to comprehend, as it hides in the lost sense of direction upon witnessing the completion of a piece of your existence - graduation, promotion, anniversary, accolade. Each a reason for celebration, yet a reason embalmed in mourning, anchored down with the vastness of vacuum that it brings with you, even as that vacuum has spare room for new musings and experiences - anxiety weighs the heaviest when it's tied to the unknown. Sometimes autumn is an April day that has waken up too early and disoriented wandered into the midst of November - a mistimed prophet parting the crispy sea of the numbed autumn air, making way for the warmth that is not yet to come... a soft intrusion of the most welcome kind...

Iced cotton candy ripped by wind;
starry air densed into sapphire; ruthless wave cuts into sleepy stones;
November.

In its attempt to make up for all that abundance of sadness, the autumn sun has the most tender and caring touch of them all. It embraces everything in its soft glow - a lover saying goodbye and tracing the shape of its love with the fingertips, barely touching it, yet absorbing every fragile detail like it's the last, the only, one. In the summer, the sun is allowed to touch the Earth freely, and in the winter, it just reaches for it in vain. Which is why it spends the entire fall saying goodbye.

Like seeing a rainbow for the first time,
with pure wonder,
one day I had the pleasure of learning
that my mind is capable of healing.

Like waking from my first nightmare,
with careful relief,
one day I learned with grief and joy
that my mind is capable of forgiving
itself.

SCATTERED THOUGHTS OF A LOST SOUL

My whole life
I've been running from the shadows around,
creating vicious circles, losing my ground;
not moving forward,
I'm cornered and dormant.

Hide away –
my only goal is to hide away;
as I don't wish to fall anyone's prey.
My eyes are still closed;
so much loathe; my mind dozed.

Don't give up.
Whatever it is, I should not give up;
pain can never make me come to a stop.
Just a little bit tired
to go on... I am tired...

Noise in head.
In my head, I hear too many voices
that are arguing over all my choices,
causing me to corrupt,
they confuse, interrupt.

Meaningless.
I tend to burn out like a wooden match;
to not give up is a habitual catch.
Same old frozen image –
I'm stuck in this scrimmage.

And maybe...
All of this is just self-illusion;
and I needn't fight with the confusion...

May my fears catch up -
I won't flee or erupt;
it's time to dare, live without care...

...It's no end.
to meet the fears is just the beginning -
need to grasp why, to them, I was clinging,
why I feared the light
for so long, tried to fight.

Fight alone.
All alone, I keep abreast the current;
but my mistakes need no more warrant,
and I can decide
what to feel, what to hide.

And some day,
when my life at last is void of rushing,
and solitude's no longer crushing,
I will recognize
lack of life, my demise.

But till then
I'm left to choke fears and doubts in my fist
'cause success without defeat is an empty list.
Yes, I'm very tired
but from life haven't been fired.

I will smile.
In spite of all the hardship, I will smile
because my life is not just one long trial.
Truth I will detect,
earn myself respect;
fears I'll accept, standing erect.

HOW MANY

How many minds   does it take   to enjoy   a piece of art
to call it worthy?

How many hearts   should be touched   by a single life
to make it meaningful?

How many smiles   does one need
to feel better?

How many actions   should be made
to bring the biggest change?

How many moments   does one miss
to cause the deepest regret?

How many words   should be free of   consideration   to damage one's
mood?   Mind?   Heart?   Soul?   Life?

And how many acts of kindness
would it require to start healing the damage?

One.

*...All it takes is just one word, one touch, one moment -
the first one, the last one, the missed one...
And all I need is just one...
    Reason to smile, reason to cry,
    Reason to love without saying goodbye,
    Reason to feel, reason to stay,
    Reason to live in my own way...*

SCARS

Two were lying on a porch,
bathing in the summer sun,
sending soap bubbles
to dance around their heads:
a boy asked a girl looking at her knees,
"What's that?"
She laughed and shook her head,
"It's a little sweet reminder
of my third day roller-skating;
a tip for you - don't skate downhill in a dress,
when you don't know how to stop."

Two were sitting on a branch
having climbed the tallest tree
in the autumn-scented park,
a vortex of colors warming their eyes:
a boy asked a girl looking at her hands,
"What's that?"
Pride read in her glance, as she answered,
"That's my many hours of practice -
you know sometimes stubbornness
can make up for talent absent."

Two were standing in the night,
and soap bubbles froze to flakes
of laughing silver shimmering in the air,
as winter breathed them out and around:
a boy asked a girl looking at her clothes,
"What's that?"
She lit up twinkling merrily,
"A pinch of green and a sprinkle of red,
mixed in with white, make for a simple recipe
for making others smile,
as they spot you in the crowd."

Two were walking hand in hand
on the path lined up with tulips,
and spring caressed their cheeks
with the softest touch of wind:
a boy asked a girl looking in her eyes,
"What's that?"
Her irises hid beneath her lashes,
"I call her Tristitia - she likes to visit,
when I least expect, and water my eyes,
and slow my plans, and make me question
the meaning of everything."

Two were falling in the sky,
each other finding and losing,
feeling nothing of the time,
as it burned through their souls
and left scars on their faces:
a boy asked a girl looking in her heart,
"What's that?"
Her face all earnest measured his,
"It's an accolade for my success
to get up and recover,
to heal and then live on -
the scars I wear with honor,
as to acquire them I paid a lot,
those badges of my strength...
You see, simple lessons are costly,
when learned too late,
and some costs are better
never repaid."

Two were two in what they were,
yet in each other, two were one.

ENOUGHNESS

i don't dislike to be so tired
as to lose my inhibitions
but i don't like to be so tired
as to spread the gloom around me

i don't dislike to cry in sympathy
at a story in a book
but i don't like to cry in sympathy
for myself since it rarely feels deserved

It's only when I've depleted myself completely out of all energy, physical and emotional, that there remains no
fuel to sustain the tension between my inner prosecutor and defender;
and in the absence of that tension rises a tender feeling of sufficiency, of enoughness,
which says "what I do is enough; what I am is enough; already enough; already just right";
and there's nobody remaining in my tired interior to negate that.

It's exhilarating. And it's rare in its exhilaration.

So, no wonder that my mind, wishing to put a temporary end to my own inner wars, grinds me down between
anxiety and depression, exhausting me to the point, where I have zero energy left to keep up the inner conflict
and supply ammunition to the sludge-tinted soldiers within.

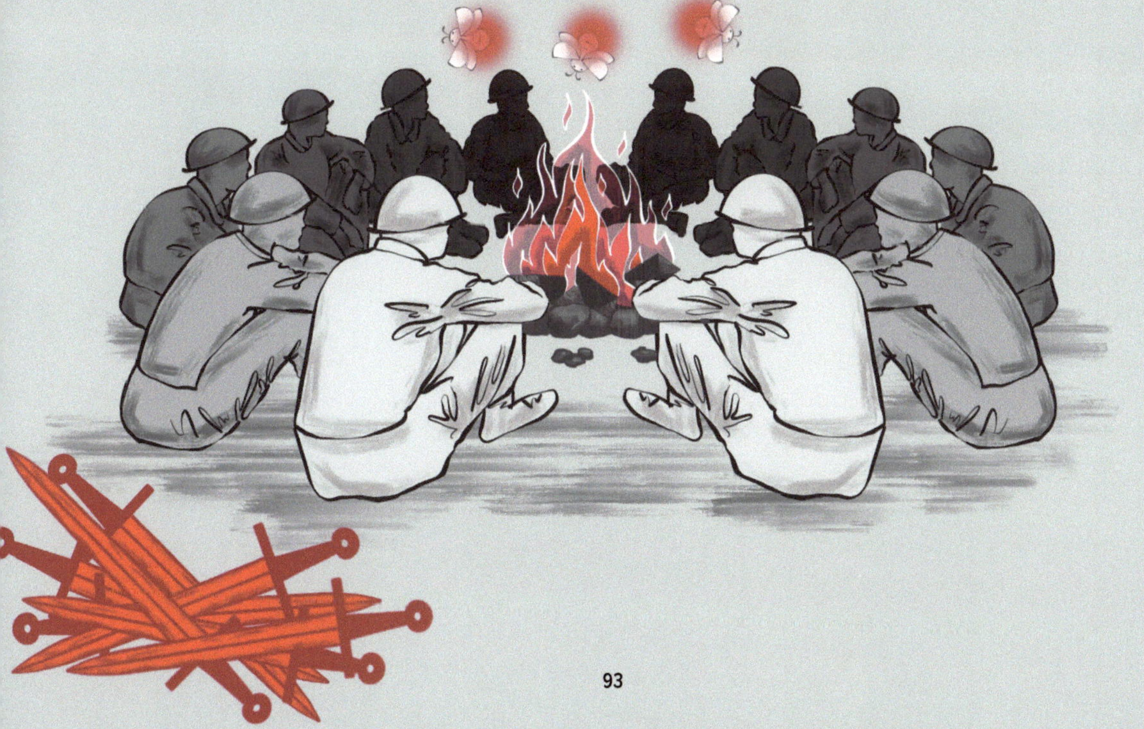

THAT WHICH LOVED YOU ALWAYS

If you look inwards, deep under the surface of what once looked like a heart,
in the far away corner of your hardened soul and numbed mind,
you will find me -

me, who's been with you through all the pulses of gravity;
me, who's been resined to your side even when you couldn't see me.

Sometimes you become deaf to my pleas,
but your inability to perceive my presence does not erase the fact of it.

I snuggled you, when you nurtured thoughts of nonexistence,
each thought a tiny parasite that you let feed on you without hesitation.
I lulled you into kindness you didn't think you deserved,

when the perceived hollow of your existence invited the slugs of despise -
your will to change covered in slime,
and with change too slippery to grasp, it felt right to suffer.

I wiped your cheeks when vultures of self-loathing infested your orbit,
and you thought the best way to deal with them was to silence
your bleats for help and stand exposed -

better be devoured than become a burden,
better be lacerated than let others see the bedlam you are.

I unsheathed my scowl to shield you only to learn I had none,
as you stared at everyone's backs, and empathized
with their rejection, justified them;

I pondered if absence of hatred counted as love,
when you said it was a relief that love didn't have to equate to "like",
as to not dislike was the gentlest thing you mustered to feel for yourself;

I wept with cheer when you emitted sunshine from your face,
forgetting that you were supposed to be a wretched storm cloud.

I prayed for you to stay in your sunny constellations for as long
as could be allowed by the theory of relativity, in which happiness
accelerated the world to the speed of light, so that your joy became the only constant.

I cringed when soaking in the bog of your pain, you'd let it splash
onto those around, or when the cold molasses of that bog embalmed
your sloth or lack of sensitivity with the soothe of false excuse.

I gasped at your insecurity, each time you crumbled into sorries and questions,
each crumb a splinter that instead of guiding you to safety
served as a stake to which you'd impale your heart, like when you asked

if one could love herself less for realizing she was incapable of loving herself more.
I awarded you your first badge of recovery when you looked in the mirror without disgust.
I thanked heaven and hell when you whispered that you didn't wish to hurt anymore,

as you claimed this year to be the year you would learn to love yourself,
and it became the year you learned to not disdain yourself
(most of the time) - it was a very good year.

I theorized whether love was hiding in wonders or wanders,
as I watched you wonder what you could possibly do to deserve to be happy;
as I watched you wander in the pursuit of happiness you didn't think you deserved.

I denied gravity through each quake of your relapses,
as I tried to sew the fissures together with promises of their temporariness,

although all you heard was that the breaks between relapses were doomed
to be finite as well, and you would dive headfirst into a crack in my sawing to hide from that truth.

I've been the tiniest fragment of you that loved you the most.
And maybe I too don't like you sometimes, but I've always loved you regardless.

I only hope that some day my tiny fragment should become your whole.

CHOICE TO KEEP TRYING

And I tried,
I tried,
to be someone I could love,
someone
I could be proud of,
someone enough;
but it was always
a condition
that for me to love me
I shouldn't be me.

And I tried,
I tried,
to be the girl I wanted to be
to reach that image, set it free;
and I tried,
but always I
failed.

Still I try,
will still try,
to pick me up
from each fall:
my pieces scatter,
maybe I'll never
gather them all;

but it doesn't matter -
I've learned to love me
with nothing at all;
I've learned to love me
for nothing at all.

CHANGE

The wind has changed at last,
and now it's a magic carpet in service of the sun,
delivering warm kisses of sunshine to each face,
swirling around, curiously sniffling everyone,
like a playful puppy welcoming new guests,
even though it is the one visiting;
at last, the wind has changed.

The tide has turned at last,
demobilizing young waters summoned for adult wars,
letting them regain their paused innocence once more,
soft shimmering waves roll over each other,
in a kids' game of leapfrog, with froth bunnies
hopping across them in a playful chase;
at last, the tide has turned.

With a glance cast so far,
with a sail full of change,
longing to learn who we are
by accepting the strange;
with the mind full of dreams,
and with hope in the heart -
no need to be perfect and prim,
it only takes brave to restart.

MORNING

Murmur of the water,
like chanting echoes of the stars
waving their farewells
lightyears away from here,
before, at last, they cease existing -
red giants turning to white dwarfs,
in a shy and quiet blast,
in a fatal collapse,
sending waves of mournful silence
all across the universe,
before finding a voice
in the murmur of the water
beneath this bridge.

Soft morning mist
covers each exposed piece of skin
with gentle kisses,
like a newborn nibbling
on his mother's chest,
affection candid in each touch -
pure innocence expresses love
in a way that passion never could;
respect and trust emerged as one
from the one who's yet to learn
the hollow meaning of either;
all the caress of a waking world's greeting
disguised in a myriad of kisses
by the soft morning mist.

Home is where I can lose
all of me, and yet find
more than I lost
because
whatever it is that I lose
wasn't me
and everything that I find
is the me
that I looked for.

LETTER TO MY PAST SELVES

*When was the last time   that you directed your eyes   at the ripples on the water
and wondered,   how they're just like echoes   of your younger little past self,
reaching to remind you   that you forgot of your dreams?*

My dear past selves, let me show you that your pain and sacrifice weren't in vain - let me share the things I know and am today because of you. I'm writing this with gratitude, and I hope that you might read this with pride. In the years leading to now, on your way to becoming me, you'll have learned:

Perfection is an unattainable illusion, and that's what makes it a perfect excuse for inaction. So you decided to stop waiting for a *perfect* moment, when you're *perfectly* ready to share your *perfect* creations with the world and started to embrace your imperfections. My dear, you stopped expressing yourself in order to be evaluated by others, and started to express yourself because that is what it means to be you. Completely and unapologetically you. After all, doing something imperfectly is better than perfectly not doing it. And the more you accept your right for imperfect self-expression, the less you judge others who exercise that right.

***

The flaws you see in others are the flaws you don't accept in yourself. Yet the reverse turns out to be true as well - the beauty you admire in others also exists within you. That is still your favorite lesson to learn.

***

You learned that it was possible to feel sorry for yourself for hating yourself and then hate yourself even more for feeling sorry for yourself. You learned that your repetitive thoughts about being tired of life despite being so young, your feelings of desperate terror at the prospect of another 50-70 years of this life, your hopeful curiosity about finding a valid way to "go" are called suicidal ideation and, apparently, not everybody has them. Those contemplations of "valid" ways to go that would excuse you for going: jumping in front of a gun to save a stranger or pushing someone out of a car's way, with you, obviously, ending up blue and cold in all cases. Perceiving every day as a struggle, you still felt guilty for wanting it to end, and so instead you imagined all the ways in which you'd be justified to go. Yet through all that, you came to learn that there is nothing wrong with looking at death as a relief, when in pain - in a twisted way, not being afraid to die helps to not be afraid to live, even in the world where life doesn't have meaning, outside of the one you imbue it with. So instead of trying to find a meaning, you started to create it, and suddenly, you found yourself living a meaningful life by infusing every aspect of it with a meaning of your choice. That was liberating too.

***

Your capacity for change is infinite, but your subconscious focus is skewed towards the terrors, so you ought to regularly apply effort to direct your conscious attention to the wonders. The slower you live, the more you live. Aggression is contagious, but so is kindness - the choice is yours.

***

The brain strives for congruency, which is a manifestation of the confirmation bias, and as such, it will do all it can to create the reality to match its convictions. And since convictions sometimes manifest as fears, it is unsurprising that you regularly found yourself in conditions that realized those fears. You lived convinced that good days would always be followed by dark days, teaching yourself to expect the arrival of the dark days, and starting to fear your good days because they became the harbinger of the dark days. Creating your own self-fulfilling prophecies. You've also lived in the world that you were convinced had no place for you, so you didn't even try to look for or create such a place. Until you knew better. Because between simple and complex, the brain tends to choose familiar, so eventually, you, my love, started to regularly practice desirable to make it more familiar. After all, the brain is capable of magic - it can make fantasies a reality, it can notice and go for opportunities you desire, it can change itself, and it is even capable of happiness.

***

You learned the importance and the value of living in the reality, even if you still long for your illusions. You learned to want to believe in what is true, abandoning wishful thinking because what is true is already so, and embracing it is less energy-consuming than rejecting it. It's also less energy-consuming to live in the reality than to sustain a fantasy.

***

Self-love used to seem impossible, especially since it's hard to love someone you don't even like. But you found a way around it: turns out, you can harness brain's aspiration for congruency - if you do things to or for yourself that you consider an expression of love, then eventually, your brain won't have a choice but designate yourself as a lovable, and even likable, person, since why else would there be acts of love towards this person. Loving through action before loving through feeling. Love as a choice rather than a happenstance.

***

In your pursuit of lightness, you rejected yourself as you were then - which wasn't light - but this self-rejection wasn't bringing you any closer to the lightness. After all, heaviness isn't to be rejected - it's to be honored.

***

Your adulthood is a continuous strive towards a confident and calm version of yourself that conjures the world around her through willful self-respect - the one that embodies the present moment, fills it with herself by attending to others as part of her curiosity, and feels her own sufficiency within all that; the one that stays present with her emotions, notices them, accepts them, along with any discomfort they bring, choosing to feel and observe them without judgement. Living shame-free used to be a dream, and now you live it.

***

You used to confuse calmness with numbness and get unnecessarily frightened, trying to get yourself to experience, to feel, those familiar inner perturbations because without them it was eerily quiet within you. And such quietude wasn't something you were used to or knew how to deal with or even felt safe in. If you were not at an emotional high - good or bad - how could you know you were alive? So you used to prefer suffering to dullness. But you learned to see peace in the mundane: after all, healthy love is calm and quiet and even boring, and so you learned to love yourself in a boring mundane way. Thank you for that.

***

It's okay and even natural to have periods of low energy and interest, to not want anything - that's how the brain recovers from overstimulation. Everyone's speed of recovery is different, so you're under no obligation to strive for someone else's norm - just pay attention to discover your own.

***

While it's scary to trust the world around you, what is even scarier is to live an unobserved and unshared life. These fears are in direct opposition with each other, so one has to give in. You can't control whether someone betrays you. But you learned that you'd be okay if they do. You'll manage. You'll get through it. Every day things would get a tiny bit better, lighter, warmer, even if in the moment you can't see it. You will be okay. That's a promise. Sometimes it's not about controlling yourself better but about trusting yourself more.

***

Depression does not define you. Anxiety does not define you. You are not a depressed and anxious person - you're a person that flirts, deals, and lives with depression, anxiety, and their derivatives. Yes, they have been your regular companions since you were at least nine years old. Yes, you were even younger when at night you felt compelled to regularly check if parents were breathing, terrified that if you broke your routine, something terrible could happen to them. But terror and pain don't define you either. Yes, they changed you, but you, my dear, learned to decide on the vector of that change. And it was only after you stopped fighting depression and anxiety as your worst enemies that you were able to spot in them those shadow parts of yourself that you stubbornly suppressed and avoided. Only when you looked at self-hatred and auto-aggression with curiosity were you able to see in them signals - signals of fears, signals of unmet needs and unconscious desires, signals of crossed boundaries. Signals and also reminders - to be attentive and gentle with yourself, to approach yourself with love and respect, looking at the parts of you that are hurting with compassion and kindness, asking them what it was that they were trying to tell you. And you'll be proud to know, that you at last learned to not just care for yourself but to *want* to take care of yourself. It took you time to get here, but it's a good place to be.

***

It's okay to reveal your depressed messy self to others - your people will have an easier time finding you when you are not wearing masks, and they happen to accept and like you just the way you are; while not-your people will get to leave and stop wasting your energy on sustaining those relationships.

***

Everything is a choice, whether or not you're aware of it. Some choices are conscious and some aren't; some are grounded in actions, and some are manifested through inaction. Still, the moment you finally saw that everything was a choice was the moment you stopped being an NPC in the game of your life. And whether you like it or not, there's no going back. It's not something you can unknow - you can fight it, you can hate it, but what is true is already so, and resistance requires quite a bit of energy, so it's better to just give in to the changes that this knowledge will bring to our life. Because the moment you learned that everything was a choice was the moment you claimed authorship of your own life. That's when you learned to look at your circumstance and instead of beating yourself up for their undesirable aspects, you started to ask yourself what choices have led here and what was the objective behind those choices - not to shame but to learn. My love, you are NOT a casualty of your circumstances, incompetence, poor planning, inattentiveness, mistakes, or whatever else might come to mind - *you* create your life, and the more you are aware of your unconscious choices and objectives driving those choices, the more influence you can exert over them.

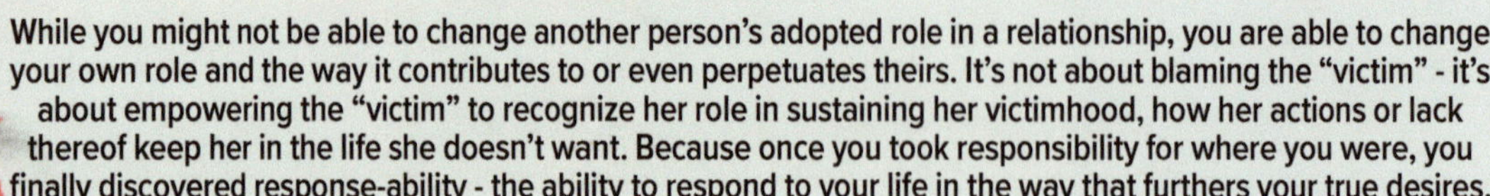

***

While you might not be able to change another person's adopted role in a relationship, you are able to change your own role and the way it contributes to or even perpetuates theirs. It's not about blaming the "victim" - it's about empowering the "victim" to recognize her role in sustaining her victimhood, how her actions or lack thereof keep her in the life she doesn't want. Because once you took responsibility for where you were, you finally discovered response-ability - the ability to respond to your life in the way that furthers your true desires.

***

It's okay to disappoint and to feel disappointed - expectations should be regularly checked and aired. Life doesn't exactly tend to follow your plan. Which makes expectations, along with comparisons, the enemy of happiness. Gratitude is the language of happiness, and you learned to speak it even towards yourself.

***

You learned that a big source of your despair - that no matter how you should live your life, there is no way to live it that wouldn't be filled with regret and sorrow and disappointment - is also a source of freedom. Because if no matter what you do, what decisions you make, or which path you choose, you'll be disappointed, then disappointment becomes a constant and can be ignored. After all, by the time you are me, you'll have already made the biggest mistake and gained the biggest regret and disappointment of your life - all other regrets will be dwarfed by it. And while the pain of this regret will haunt us for a long time, it also provides a twisted liberation because no other mistake could ever eclipse that one. So we can go around trying and erring, knowing that our worst mistake has already been made. In the end, we are made more of our mistakes than of our successes because the pain of mistakes weighs more than the joy of successes, but you don't need to dwell on the former - just reflect on your lessons and move on.

***

What happened, happened necessarily - it had to happen based on the circumstances that precipitated the events around it. There's lessons to learn but no use for shame. Freedom to do anything is often desired but misunderstood - for when you can do anything, it becomes hard to pick something to do. Limitation, in moderation, can give direction and even inspire creativity.

***

Darling, you learned that everyone, including you, experiences this life for the first time, and we are all figuring it out at our own individual pace. So when some say that the right thing is the harder one, and others claim that the right thing should be easy, you learned to think for yourself and to look for a third (and fourth, and fifth) alternative. You learned to not just ask questions, but to have fun with them, with you favorite question being "What for?" If the natural inclination of the heart is for darkness, should it really be forced into the light under someone else's premise of that being what's best for it? Are virtues really worth more if they don't come easy, if one has to work for them? And what is then the worth of natural kindness, if it's not a conscious choice to resist some known evil? Should you care about anything and everything or just what matters to you? And what if you want to but can't care? Is a human being defined by the degree of caring or is that degree defined by a human being? How to revive something that has died in you, if you don't really know what it is and where it's located? And worse, if you constantly have to force yourself to care about reviving that something?

***

Very few people live their lives harboring harmful intentions towards you. So you learned to assume positive intent behind others' actions, or at least the absence of malicious intent, which made your life lighter. The world is just a projection of what you reflect into it.

***

Regret is a form of self-resentment. It's resenting yourself for not having made a different choice, and holding on to that resent. And there are few things that age worse than unaddressed resentment, as it will brew into passive (or even active) auto- (and, eventually, outer-) aggression. After all, living with or being part of someone that you hold deep resentment against can be hellish - few of us are gracious enough to remain fair, unbiased, caring, and gentle towards someone we hold grudges against, even if, or especially when, that someone is us. There could even be a desire for justice, a need, an urge to engage in revenge, to punish. And it can create for such a complex internal conflict, in which instead of ensuring forward or present looking changes, we direct our attention at holding on to the past and beating ourselves over the head in a form of self-punishment. And regret *is* a form of self-punishment. It's a cruel inner adult inflicting the pain of being unable to change the past on a child that didn't know better. So you, my dear, learned to show compassion to the child. You also learned that regret is not a driving force for change - it actually can undermine and hinder your aspirations for better/different lives for yourself. Still it can serve as a signal of wanting a difference. A lesson to not let your perceived shouldn't's turn into forced wouldn't's and then into regretful couldn't's. To not be afraid to try something new, remembering that you regret more the things that you didn't do.

***

It is possible to be afraid that no change will ever be big enough to make a difference and still move forward towards yet another life experiment. Commitment is the preamble for change.

***

You're a small universe, and you learned to take time to discover its beautiful secrets. You learned to see your heart as a little bird that is flapping its wings in fearful agitation against the cage of your chest every time when you got angry or frustrated with yourself. And that helped spark self-compassion by placing your hands on your chest and focusing on calming the little creature with soothing words and thoughts. That innocent little bird wishes for your happiness and desires your love - so you learned to take care of it, for it's always there for you.

***

You are who you are. Here. Now. So you learned to not disrespect yourself by wishing to be somebody else. Instead, you take deep breaths and follow the movement of the air passing through your lungs, and how with it, your life moves in a never ending dance. My love, please, never forget to be part of this dance.

***

If you think you can do something, you are right. If you think you can't do something, you are right. Pick wisely, but also remember, that you can do it. I know you can do it because I've already done it.

***

You're worthy of being loved. You're worthy of the love that you desire. You deserve to be happy.

***

You were born with inherent value - nobody, even yourself, can ever take that away from you. The value of your life can only go up. Even when you feel worthless, trust me, you contain multitudes within you, and each one is valuable. After all, even the tiniest bug can find a leaf that will feel its presence and wobble under its weight.

***

The highest degree of presence is not being in the moment but rather being the moment. Reaching the complete integration between your self and the world around you.

***

It's a beautiful time, where you are now, and you have the right to enjoy it. Be open to the transient beauty of each passing moment. Remember that when I need to feel better, I take myself to you.

***

I will not shame my past self for not knowing better.

***

I love you. I love myself. I love my life. I love people I have at my side. I'm learning constantly. I'm evolving with each experience. I know how to be my authentic self, without excuses or regrets. I can always do better, and I will, but not because I'm not already enough, but because I respect myself too much to not at least give it a try.

***

Thank you for always looking out for magic, for finding magic all around you, and for creating it when it's not easily available.

***

You might be surprised to know that my ideal version of me is you.

LIFE

Ah, how often do we forget to raise our head and look around...
The world's so pretty! Let's not be fretting about the small things that just don't count.
When was the last time we looked at the sky and really saw it, really felt it?...
Life passes quick - let us at least try to live every moment and not spare any bit!

Oh life, thank you for all that you're giving me:
The beauty of waking up and feeling that there's still something left to feel;
The rise of the sun after each moment of darkness I find myself in;
The touch of the warmth in the coldest moment of my existence;
The breath, the shake, the calm before the quake and right after it.

Oh life, my sweet beautiful child,
my gracious ancient lady,
thank you for holding me in your arms,
thank you for letting me hold you in mine.

ONLY AT NIGHT

Only at night,
I have no fear
that someone discovers the tears
I hide.

Only at night,
having embraced
myself with the darkness I face,
I turn off the light.

Only at night,
I'm losing myself:
to find my senses, I'm forced to delve,
and so I fight.

Only at night,
I set myself free,
confessing my sins, revealing my dreams,
making everything right.

It is only at night,
I have no fear
that someone discovers the true me
inside.

WHAT IF

*But what if I don't need to search for happiness? What if...I'm already happy?...
What if...I've been happy this entire time and just stubbornly refused to see it, to admit it?...*

I recently caught myself remembering some delightful spring mornings, when I sat on the windowsill of my childhood bedroom and read "Harry Potter and The Philosopher's Stone" for the 27th time, with sunshine caressing my face, birds chirping in the background cacophony of an open window, and the curtains playing waves with the wind - a magical combination of being in the state of flow and also at peace... Somehow, for the longest time I've refused to admit that I have savored plenty of such lovely moments in the recent years; worse yet, I've neglected to notice happiness in those moments. I've refused to acknowledge that, maybe, I haven't actually been only unhappy and depressed - maybe, I just was too afraid, too unwilling, to accept the happiness available to me here and now, as if thinking that if I accept it, I'd be settling, and thus somehow waiving my right to have anything more... What a silly fear! And yet such a strong one...

But what if I've been going about it all wrong? What if I'm such a perfectionist that I've set an unrealistic definition for happiness - a complete and utter absence of any negative feelings or moments in life? Yet, it turns out that having those is the most normal thing - sort of a sign of a life being lived.

Happiness isn't about never feeling tired or unfulfilled or lonely; it's also not about absence of any dissatisfaction; nor is it about always liking what I do. My dislike for certain aspects of my job or occasionally overpowering weight of loneliness are just attributes of my reality, and their presence doesn't preclude happiness because *happiness is everything else.*

Happiness isn't about what I have - it's about how I choose to feel about what I have; but more specifically, it's about how what I feel about what I have compares against how I expected to feel about it. And I don't think I ever stopped to think of my criteria for recognizing a happy life...

Happiness isn't some massive moment of joy - it's the aggregation of all the moments of peace, excitement, anticipation, pride, pleasure, flow, and so much more; and no, it's not about forcing myself to find joy in the mundane - it's about realizing that mundane is in the perception and I have a choice for how to see it. And it's okay to want more - I want to want more - but I also want to appreciate what I have.

I feel light. And I am ready and willing to be happy in the here and now, leaving behind the existential dread of settling for too little happiness or for too small a reason for happiness or for some insufficient level of achievement to be happy with.

I feel change. And I feel also how I resist that change - old habits not just peeking but clawing through. Although the curious thing I couldn't help noticing was that by holding myself to lower standards, I've been able to do better and grow more.

What if the dark places I used to send myself down to were just the safest places to hide at the time, and now I have no need for them anymore?

Ilana Kovalle: Ode to Hope and Despair
You
are
a beautiful thing!

You're
my
favorite
beautiful thing!

You're
such
a beautiful thing -

The whole world is better
since it's got
you in.

107

EXCUSES

«Too late to start»
«Too little support»
«I tried, but I failed»
«I'll always fall short»

«I could never be good»
«Too much at stake»
«I'm okay, where I am,
Even though I'm a fake»

«Under too much stress»
or simply «Not blessed»
«I would but right now
my life is a mess»

«I need someone else
to guide me to my dream,
if that person's not here -
it's not meant to be»

But, if only, later, unless -
so many reasons
to not try our best;
later, unless, if only, but –
«I wish but for this
I'm simply not cut»

Stop making excuses!
Our decisions WE own.
Inaction's a sin
I refuse to condone.

ODE TO MY PUPPY

My therapist told me to cry every day for two weeks;

and this morning my coffee was ruined - too salty.

Coffee is supposed to be black but mine never is, just like black holes

aren't exactly black - not letting the light escape, they are simply without color.

And if black holes suck everything in, yet destroy it in the process,

should they be considered as filled with emptiness?

My heart was one of such black holes - an emptiness so overwhelming

that it swallowed everything to fill itself,

yet an emptiness so abysmal that it overwhelmed

everything it swallowed, dissolving it in itself, unfillable.

My body couldn't stretch, so the density of the emptiness within

began to grow, until under the pressure of my physical limits,

it started to fuse, and fuse it did into salt,

letting the excesses slip out of my eyes, ruining my coffee.

I sought to cry because crying should offer release.

Like bleeding a patient in the medieval times,

tears are supposed to let the bad stuff out.

Although crying better help more than bleeding.

So I cried. And I cried. And I cried.

I knew I was mourning something with those tears.

The life I had. The life I wanted to have.

The life I couldn't have. The life I'd never have.

Which one? All of them?

The first time I picked up your trembling body,

your tiny head cradled into the nook under my chin;

the moist air of your human-like long exhale tickled my neck with unfamiliar warmth;

it took me a moment to realize that I too exhaled with relief into your neck - a relief of mutual acceptance.

I cried again a few days after you came.

With you, overwhelmingness became a feeling from the outside. It was a peculiar change.

Like adding cilantro to a salad - first it's too much, then you can't seem to have enough.

Each night you snuffled in my ear, your tiny heater of a body emitting the love I never dared to hope for.

So yes, a few days after you came, I still cried. And again, they were tears of mourning.

I didn't know it yet, but this time I was grieving my depression,

Grieving for the pain of my past self, hoping I wasn't betraying her with my healing.

A few days after you came, I cried, mourning. For one last time.

you're wonderful
you're worthy
you're loved
you deserve
"Forgive me."
"I forgive you."
"Forgive me."
"I forgive you."
"Forgive you."
"I forgive y... me?"
"Forgive you."
"I forgive... me...
I... forgive me.
I forgive me.
I forgive me."

SMILE

As I try to stretch my very thoughts into the shape of a smile,
it surprises me how unnatural, how uneasy, that feels.

When did my mind turn into a sanctuary of negativity?
No, when did I allow it to exile positive thoughts?
To associate them with lost hopes, to cloak them in derision over their childishness?
When did I accept that all I deserve is to fail in all of my tryings?
When did I start condemning myself to failures by stopping to even try?
When did I begin to deceive myself that I know the future and in it I've lost?

Questioning my habitual negativity, allowing these very thoughts to emerge in my mind feels so unfamiliar that I catch my head shaking from side to side, as if in a subconscious attempt to reclaim the negativity. And as I'm repainting the patterns in my mind into the hues I believed forgotten, a new thought strikes at me with its soft colorful glow, to which my mouth knows only one way of responding - smiling.

"I've seen the future, and in it I'm happy."

...when I looked up
the hand that held me
was mine...

ACKNOWLEDGMENTS

I want to express gratitude to my wonderful family and friends, who have supported me in every crazy endeavor.

I'd also like to specifically thank a few people that had a more direct impact on this book:

• Melissa Sussens, for your patient, thoughtful, considerate, and attentive editing;

• Tatyana Takushevich, for your incredible work on the illustrations and for helping me bring my vision to life;

• Larisa Parfentieva, for bringing me into the world of book publishing and introducing me to Tanya and to our writing group;

• Мою прекрасную писательскую группу: Алина, Марина, Марина, Света, Алена, Ксюша, Мила, Катя, Дария, Маша, Таня, и Таня - девочки, спасибо за то, что вдохновили и показали, что своя книга это вполне себе осуществимо;

• Bostjan Lisec, for believing in the feasibility of this project and taking on the challenge of helping me befriend the illustrations with the text in the way that compliments both;

• Megan Falley and the course "Poems That Don't Suck," for liberating me to write unapologetically, for expanding my capacity for poetic expressions, and for challenging me to take my writing to the next level:

> *Poems written in Megan's class: "a Few Signs Something Is Wrong," "Strength, a Matter of Definitions," "Writing a Love Letter to Myself," "That Which Loved You Always," and "Ode to My Puppy";*

• Andrea Gibson, Sabrina Benaim, Neil Hilborn, and Sarah Kay for every gut punch by your words that left me craving more, for introducing me to so many intricate shapes that poetry can take, for the inspiration;

• Ameerah, Summer, Nancy, Smooches and the Revising Out Loud community, for the beautiful space of respect and acceptance to share and experiment with my writing;

• Liza, Swosti, Francesca, Ryan, JY, Nadya, Gail, Vanessa, for interacting with my writing and being some of the first people to ever hear about and actually see early drafts of this collection (and being supportive about my intentions to publish it some day);

• Anthony, for showing so much appreciation for and interest in my writing that it inspired me to write more; for proving that one significant reader can be all a writer might ever need; for being my main audience for the longest time; for demonstrating that it takes acknowledgment by one person to make a piece of writing worth all effort; for being the first and primary reader for most of my writing; for motivating me to write with mere anticipation of sharing that writing with you.

ABOUT THE AUTHOR

IlanaKovalle is a writer, poet, and songwriter, currently residing in Jersey City. Her life started in a large family in a small village of rural Kazakhstan, where she secretly wrote poems, songs, and stories since the age of seven. Secretly because with no musical background or formal poetry education, that little girl believed her "not good enough" creations had no right to be shared. It all changed, when IlanaKovalle moved to the United States and started to slowly explore the world of expressive art forms. It dawned on her that with self-expression being a form of communication, few things were more tragic than under-communication or not shared self-expression. In the end, "good enough" was a myth, a procrastination strategy, a defense mechanism, or just an excuse - as long as she desired something, she was already good enough to at least start doing it. She has been on a mission to inspire and support other self-doubting creators to give themselves permission to create imperfectly.

IlanaKovalle's music can be found on all musical platforms (or at the QR code below). Her short collection of poetry and prose "LOML" can be found on Amazon and Kindle, and her debut novel "Cerulean" will be published in the near future.

IlanaKovalle holds a Bachelor's degree in Business Administration and a Master's degree in Accountancy, both from the University of Wisconsin, Madison. She is also a certified well-being trainer with the Neurointegration Institute and has a positive psychology coaching certification from Positive Acorn. Her top values are Fairness, Connection, Stimulation, Forgiveness, and Authenticity.

For more information, please visit her website: www.IlanaKovalle.com